Dear Brit,

Thank you for promoting a book you didn't even read,  !

My heart is so full knowing that there are people in the world willing to take a chance and be a cheerleader for you - thank you for the team spirit, I couldn't have asked for more!

Love,
Shirrá

D1282515

LOVE AND WAR

A BWWM MODERN HISTORICAL ROMANCE

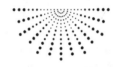

SHIRRÁ LYNN

First paperback edition February 2021

Book design by
Clare Sager

Cover Design by
Covers in Color
www.coversincolor.com

ISBN 978-1-7362249-2-2 (paperback)
ISBN 978-1-7362249-0-8 (ebook)

www.shirralynn.com

I would like to dedicate this book to the team of wonderful, creative, talented, supportive women...and men, who supported me through the many different steps it took to tell this story. I am grateful for each of you, I'd still be walking back and forth in my room, in my robe, totally confused if it wasn't for you. With all my heart, thank you!
And thanking my Lord and savior in heaven for without whom nothing would be possible, thank you Father.
...EARMUFFS!!!, lol

PREFACE

I am not a historian. Though I do love history, and learning about all the dramatic events that took place in the past. This story was actually supposed to be a prequel to another novel I was writing last year and just couldn't finish, so I put that one down and just started typing and all of a sudden I could see faces, hear conversations, feel emotions just as naturally as if they were happening to me. I got everything down on paper...or a screen in the early mornings, late at night, sometimes waking up in the middle of the night with an epiphany, during lunch breaks-basically whenever I could, the story wouldn't wait.

I did my best to follow proper dates and timelines, from the invasion/annexation of Austria to the invasion of France, maybe speeding things up a bit and giving allowances for minor details for artistic license to make the story flow a little better, but I think we're okay. Names of my characters I researched for days, going through individual meanings, geographical locations and how a name would best represent a character, then I strung them together to fit each personality.

This story isn't that fantastical, it's actually plausible -

people find love in strange ways and odd places, and this love develops over short or long lengths of time, they lose love sometimes in the same way. And that is what this book is about, exploring *Love and War* between lovers, *Love and War* between friends, *Love and War* between families and countries, it's all interwoven. Glean from this story what you will, but I hope in doing so, you will enjoy your time visiting with this set of characters and falling into their world if only for a moment, just as much as I did.

We collide,

Melting, blending, achieving

A greater devotion of love than ever mastered before.

We topple,

Struggling, twisting, climbing

Making our way back to each other over and over again.

No one...

No-thing, can come between us...

We are one.

Forever and for always.

-Shirrá Lynn

A VISIT

In a small car
On a long road
A daughter drives to a big house

CALIFORNIA | 1980

Lily

I turn on my left flasher before turning into the driveway of my childhood home. My third childhood home to be exact. My family and I came to America when I was 12. Though it was a huge culture shock for us growing up in a predominantly white American neighborhood, we were used to being different. So, the shock wore off quickly; for us anyway.

It was rough. The '50s and '60s weren't exactly kind, but things eventually got better, and it didn't hurt that my family had money. I learned early that in America, the color of money trumps skin tone almost every time, at least superficially. Let's be honest, as a child sometimes a little superficial pacification goes a long way to keep smiles on faces and tears unshed. Get called "nappy-headed," enough times at school, buy the school...how's that for pacification, worked for me.

I park in the large round driveway and push open the car door with all my might. It's a little difficult these days because I'm eight months pregnant. Let me tell you, being pregnant is no fun, though Maman [*mommy*] tried to convince me otherwise. She told me how much she *looooved* being pregnant with me and my brothers, and like a fool, I believed her stories-- until it actually happened to me. The fifth time I threw up is when I figured that all mothers tell their daughters that pregnancy is grand, if only to secure at least one grand-child out of her daughter's union. If mothers told their daughters the truth about swollen ankles, throwing up morning, noon, and night, tender breasts, and fifty trips to the bathroom a day, no woman would be so inclined to get pregnant. Civilization as we know it would end. On second thought, just to preserve the human race, I'll probably tell my daughter the same thing Maman told me.

As I scoot my way out of the car, our maid Lisette makes her way to me with her arms flung wide. She has been with us since before we moved to the States. Though now in her late 60's, Lisette is still very much a stunning woman with dark carob skin, and platinum hair pulled back into a sleek chignon. Both my brothers had crushes on her growing up, which, to their dismay, she gracefully ignored.

"Belle!" Her smile is bright and welcoming, yet I return her loving expression with a smirk.

"Oh, s'il te plaît! Je ressemble à un tank!" [*Oh, please, I look like a tank!*]

Lisette slaps my arm and scolds me, while at the very same time rubbing my swollen tummy.

"Ferme ta bouche fille, le bébé peut t'entendre et tu lui donneras un complexe avant sa naissance. Je devrais te frapper!" [*Shut your mouth girl, the baby can hear you and you'll give him a complex before he's born. I should smack you!*]

She commences to pop me on the bottom, and I cover it with my hands, laughing.

"Non, Madame, nooooonn!"

She laughs and kisses my cheeks, then with a slim finger points upward to the second floor of the house. I see my mother, Victoire, smiling and waving from the window that brightens her sitting room. That's her sacred place, the one place we were not allowed to enter when we were children. It's her own special room for her own special purposes, but as we grew older, she allowed us more and more visits. Now, as an adult, whenever I come to visit we always end up there for our little mother-daughter chats.

I follow behind Lisette into my family home. The wonderful, familiar smells and electric buzz of love fill me with familiar excitement and happiness. I waddle up the left staircase and make my way to my mother's sitting room. When I open the door, she is perched quietly in a chic and lovely peach silk pantsuit. The sun shines through the window giving her an ethereal glow.

"Bonjour Maman." I try to kiss her cheek, squatting as low as I can to reach her, but I end up right at her temple, *best I can do*.

"Bonjour mon Bébé, anglais s'il teplaît." [*Hello, my baby, English please.*]

"Vraiment!?" [*Really!?*]

"Oui, I'm in the mood," she sighs.

I chuckle at her 'mood'. When we were little, some days it was all French, other days all English and in between *those* days was German. Whichever she felt, my siblings and I were along for the ride.

I look down to see my mother smiling at gray and white pictures from her special box. The box which held all of her tiny trinkets and favorite photos of us from when we were children. We loved looking at these pictures with her growing up. But there would always come a time when the joy would end. There was one missing picture that she could never show us and that was a picture of her mother and father.

"Maman, we've looked at these many, many times," I say smiling, hoping to thwart the impending emotional upheaval.

"Oui, Chérie, but we have a new baby on the way, and I want to be able to tell them a story." She begins spreading pictures out like playing cards, placing them back and forth between us on the settee as if starting a game of memory, lining each picture up with great care.

I furrow my brows.

"What story Maman?"

She smiles mischievously, continuing to place smiles with smiles and hugs with hugs.

"An unlikely story, oui?"

I'm curious now. We've been through this box many times. There are many pictures, and many family stories, each starting with the familiar phrase, *"ah, yes that was in..."*

"Maman, all of these pictures I know. I know all the stories and so will the baby, these are all pictures of us, nothing here is unlikely...I'm confused?"

She reaches out to me and rubs her hand down my arm, then places it on my belly giving a few gentle pats.

"This is a different story, ma Chère. Sit with me while we wait for tea, and I will tell you."

I nod my head yes. I remove my shoes from my swollen

feet watching my mother as she looks wistfully at the pictures.

"It was 1940," she begins in a serious tone, "and it was time to let my voice rest after a long three months of singing in Marrakech. I had gone back home to my piedàterre in Paris, only blocks away from Maman and Papa. My parents didn't approve of me being a lounge singer, having been classically trained, but I had always dreamed of singing jazz and blues. Back then, my voice floated on the air. It was a gift. So many of my friends and peers were making their way in the world through art and music, and I joined them. Ahh, it was a lovely time, Chère, but all was to come to a stop. Over time, friends went missing, gigs began to dry up, and then came the rumors of Hitler invading Paris. The friends that remained were fleeing the city. I had even started traveling with two bodyguards while in Marrakech, I couldn't count on being safe anywhere in the world at the time.

After my friend Josephine left Paris, I knew it was time for me as well. I packed all of my things and stopped at my parents' home to beg them to come with me to the countryside. I had saved a great deal of money and was able to purchase myself a sweet little cottage back in 1936. I had painted and furnished it how I'd pleased over the years. But, my parents would hear none of it. Not only was my lifestyle an embarrassment to my father, who had worked so hard for his station as a banker, but he was also adamant that no respectable Catholic girl would spend her days roaming Europe alone, and singing in nightclubs with swarthy characters. On the other hand, Maman was surprised that the clubs even let me entertain. My mother being a quadroon woman, my skin was never to her liking. Though, surprisingly she fell deeply in love with my father, whose skin was dark as night."

My mother stretches out her arm to me and rubs her finger gently back and forth to emphasize her next point.

"I wasn't fair, I was only a brighter shade of brown. She loved me, but there were never enough pretty dresses or hot combs in the world to stop her from saying, 'you are so pretty, ma Chère, if only you were lighter'. Maybe that's why I chose my profession, to prove that the world wanted me despite my tone."

She shakes her head and chuckles, then turns to the window and stares for a while. I touch her hand as she takes in a shaky breath. "As I said," she continues, "they were uninterested in leaving. They didn't believe the rumors were true. So, I told them that I would go and set up the cottage with provisions, then come back for them the next day, but my pleadings fell on deaf ears. Could they not see all of their friends leaving!? Did they not read the papers!?"

She's shouting now, standing to her feet and crossing her arms over her chest to soothe herself. She turns to me with an apologetic gaze, and I smile gently, understanding her pain.

"I never saw them again...and this is where the story begins."

2

THE METRO

PART ONE

In a hollowed house
Blocks from the Metro
A woman searches

PARIS | JUNE 1940

Victoire

I've come back to the house to force Maman and Papa to come with me. But when I arrive, the house is empty and tossed. Our furniture, pots, pans, pictures, all sliced and turned over. I run upstairs to their room. Maman's beautiful dresses are all ripped apart, some are even missing and Papa's safe is opened and bare. The rolling sensation in my stomach is too much to take. I run from their room, down the stairs to the front door, and standing only a few feet away are at least eight SS swarming my car, admiring it, touching it, and laughing. They stand there, joking with each other proud of what they've done.

I back away slowly, making as little noise as possible, hoping their focus remains on my shining, new red coupé. Turning swiftly on my heels, I run to the back quarters near the kitchen. Not even our maid Lisette is here, laughing or cooking, or sneaking kisses with the butcher's son Jean-Marc who delivers our meat. Where have they all gone? What has happened to them? Why didn't they listen? I make my way past Maman's tiny raised garden where she and Lisette grow peppers and squashes. A slight unseasonal breeze blows the faint scent of capsicum across my face as I open our slim back gate. I turn back, to take what I fear to be, a brief last look at my family home. We were fortunate to have such a home in the city. No doubt it will soon be confiscated. If the rumors are true, our home will soon be inhabited by some Nazi officer. I cringe at the thought of my childhood home being tainted by some disgusting animal, their smell and filth seeping into our walls, but there is no time to think about that now.

My car is compromised. I have to make it somewhere safe on foot, but where? Miette's is the first place I think of. My friends and I would go there almost every night after we performed. All the waitstaff, the hosts, chef, and manager were our friends. At Miette's, there would be someplace to hide or someone to drive me back to my cottage. Maybe I will pass Maman and Papa along the way, or maybe they are already waiting for me! I gave them plain, clear directions before I left them yesterday just in case they changed their minds...yes, yes they are at the cottage, they must be at the cottage...*God please, let them be there*.

I make my way swiftly down the back alleyway away from the house, then make a sharp right onto the sidewalk. All I need to do is catch the Metro. Just a few stops and I'll be safe at Miette's. I pass face after face, making my way through the people. I keep my head down, as I split couples walking hand in hand. Looking down or up, I gather unwanted attention, but I keep moving, fast but steady. I see the sign for the Metro just two blocks away.

"Halt, schwarzes Mädchen! Wohin gehst du?" [*Stop, black girl! Where are you going?*]

The voice from behind me is piercing with malicious mischief. I don't understand him, I only speak French and English, but I comprehend what he is saying. I keep walking, hoping he won't continue speaking to me, but my hopes are dashed when I see soldiers stomping toward me. Large men in grey uniforms grab me by both of my arms, almost pulling them out of the sockets. I cry out in pain and fear but no one even dares to look, much less help me. I kick and struggle against their hold but my strength is no match for them.

Soon, I am thrown into a great mass of people huddled together in front of a long black wrought iron gate. Men, women, children mashed together, all crying and moaning, trying to argue their way back to the journey they were on just moments before they were rounded up and hauled away. I cross my arms over my chest rubbing my hands under my arms, still feeling the remnants of the strong hands that pulled at me. I grimace at what I know to be the beginning of bruises on my flesh, while I take quick glances out of the corner of my eye toward my destination.

It's so close, I think to myself, *I can make it if I run,* but just as I turn my foot in the direction of the station, four more soldiers bubble up from the underground stairs, again, laughing. I can't for the life of me understand what is so damned funny. They all seem tickled by war and the ruination of lives. My question on hilarity is soon answered when I feel a strange hand sweep across my cheek.

"Ah, eine hubsche Negerfrau." [*Ah, a pretty nigger woman.*] He and his men laugh.

I freeze, trying not to tremble, trying to keep my eyes forward on the Metro. His fingers draw a slow line from my jaw to my hair which is pressed and pinned into swoops at the nape of my neck. He wraps a finger around a curl and pulls it from the many bobby pins holding my trindles in place. I can hear the sound of my hair rubbing between his dry fingers as he looks at it with curiosity.

"Sag mir, Negerfrau, sind die Haare auf deiner Muschi so glatt und weich wie die Haare auf deinem Kopf? Sollen wir das untersuchen? Ich bin neugierig...die Bilder von Affen, die ich gesehen habe, geben mir nicht viel Anhaltspunkte. Zieh dich aus!" [*Tell me nigger woman, are the hairs on your pussy as soft and smooth as the hairs on your head? I'm curious...the pictures I see of monkeys don't give me many clues. Take off your clothes!*]

I don't understand, but again, I know I'm being commanded to do something--something that I know I'd rather not think of. My eyes dart around for someone, anyone to help me, but there is nothing...there is no one. Just as I begin to speak and ask him to explain in French, he pulls my hair hard, arching my neck back violently.

"Ich sagte, du sollst dich verdammt nochmal ausziehen!" [*I said, fucking strip!*]

The hands come again, this time pulling at my clothes, and I lose all composure. I begin to scream and kick. Some of the crowd at the wall cry out in a meek protest. One poor elderly man tries to help me but he is knocked down and receives the butt end of a gun to his temple, *thank you, old man...I won't forget your kindness.* Just as my blouse is ripped from me, a long shiny black car with flags zooms across the street blocking my view of the Metro, my only view of hope.

3

DESIRES AND DISAPPOINTMENTS

In a pink cocktail lounge
Sitting between twins
A man shifts

MARRAKECH | NOVEMBER 1939

Emil

Everything is pink. From the cushions that lay on the ground, to the pampas grass, standing tall in their clay pots. The tables are the only things that don't take on the monochromatic hue as they sit in the middle of large cushions, making them look like little gold and blue charm boxes that hold champagne goblets, and small platters of olives and dates. I shift around, trying to situate myself reasonably. I'm not used to sitting on the floor, much less on dozens of what might as well be bed pillows. My 6'3" frame barely allows my legs to fit comfortably in any position, and my cummerbund is making my pursuits worse by digging into my ribs. It cuts off what little circulation is left from my final sitting position of one leg up, and one leg down, practically lying on the floor.

I crane my neck over my shoulder and look toward the entrance of the lounge. Rolf disappeared early in the day, leaving me to entertain our 'guests' Lottie and Dottie Schneagle, the two big breasted identical twins of Herr Klaus Schneagle, a friend of Rolf's father. He knew that Rolf and I were taking this little junket to Marrakech and slipped our location to the twins. They're both fuckable. Their breasts are more like flotation devices than actual appendages, but I'm not complaining. Rolf was more or less pissed that his time was now compromised by the recent joining of the twins to our getaway.

My friend has been making more and more trips to Marrakech alone over the past two years. Once a month really. Sometimes staying for months on end doing God knows what. I decided I would come along with him this time, to his delight. But, since arriving here, I've spent most of my time alone exploring the souks, swimming in the pool, and reading to prepare for my several scheduled surgeries. I don't mind the time alone, but I thought Rolf would at least spend a night or two with me out on the town. We have been here three weeks and tonight is the first night we actually planned to go out for more than just a cup of the thick black tar that passes as coffee. Now, here I am looking over my shoulder at the door every few minutes, trying to entertain the "twin titties", and Rolf has yet to appear.

"Hey sexy," Lottie purrs in my ear.

I turn my head towards her, and I'm met with her robust cleavage. Her hand runs slowly across my neck pulling at my bow tie, loosening it. Moments later I feel another hand moving down the thigh of my raised leg, growing dangerously close to my cock. I look down and see that Lottie's other hand is filled with a cigarette holder, and my mind snaps to Dottie who must be bored waiting for Rolf. As much as a little rub and tug would be a nice treat from the twosome, Dottie is Rolf's conquest, not mine.

I grab Dottie's hand and kiss the pale, smooth skin on the back. "Are you not anxious for Rolf's arrival?" I ask her as a subtle rebuff. She rolls her eyes and huffs, moving back to where she was sitting just as Rolf joins our little party. Sweaty and disheveled, he hops over the cushions frenetically and smiles wider than a half-moon. I've noticed this energetic shift since the moment we arrived in Marrakech. My best friend has always been extremely charming, yet brooding and cynical, enjoying alcohol and the company of fast women whenever possible to drown out the voices of his mother, father, and the gossip columns. However, from the moment we stepped off the plane *this* is the Rolf I see. I like it, but can't place my finger on the source of this change. He nudges me, biting his bottom lip and pulling a bottle of champagne from his jacket, then a second out from under his arm. We all cheer, except for Dottie who is still sulking and looking at Rolf curiously.

"Wo sind Sie gewesen?", [*Where have you been?*] Dottie asks, her face scrunching as she moves closer to Rolf, sniffing at his neck. Rolf's mood changes immediately, back to his sullen brooding nature.

"Why does it matter?"

Dottie jerks back as if having been flicked on the forehead.

"...because you smell like perfume, and none that I've ever worn, or that I'm familiar with. It smells of-," before she can finish her description Rolf stands and walks over closer to Lottie, plopping himself down, and lying on his side. He turns his back to us all, focusing his attention on the stage. I halt Lottie's attack on my clothing and go sit with my friend of 30 years who is now smoking, deep in thought.

"I don't care where you've been," I say, not looking in his direction, knowing he needs a modicum of privacy for his reflections, "I just know that you're happy, and that's all that matters."

"Is it?"

Rolf's retort is venomous, yet I sit silently, also focusing on the stage. I hear the twins behind us, whispering to each other.

"I knew he was gay, why else would he not want me?" Rolf looks back over his shoulder in their direction and chuckles, shaking his head incredulously.

"Yes, your happiness is important to me."

Rolf sighs heavily. "I know--I'm sorry."

We look at each other as Dottie continues to whine. We laugh and clink our champagne bottles, taking giant swigs just when the curtain goes up on stage. I look down from my upturned bottle and almost choke on the perfumed liquid as an Angel appears on the stage before my eyes. God must have been most jealous when he sent her from heaven. In all my 36 years I have never encountered such beauty, because here it all is, amassed in one woman whose voice drifts over me like a tranquil breeze, relieving me of the heat rising in my cheeks.

Dulcet tones flow from beautifully defined lips, adorned with the most perfect cupid's bow. Her peach silk gown clings to her rounded hips and gracefully lays atop breasts that almost dare to peek through the plunging 'V' front. Marabou feathers dance as they cascade delicately down her shoulder. The lighting from above bathes her confectionary pecan skin in a golden glow, making a halo of her dark brown hair. I can see Rolf watching me from the corner of my eye, he traces my line of sight directly to the object of my desire. He leans over, placing the mouth of his bottle under my chin, moving it upward slowly and closing my gaping jaw, then he throws a napkin at my face.

"You're drooling. You should mop it up before someone slips."

And I do, with two long strokes across my mouth, zombie-like, never taking my eyes from her. All sorts of thoughts are running through my mind. *What do I say to make her smile? What story could I possibly tell her to make her laugh? How will she sound screaming my name as I make her cum over, and over again in my bed?* I halt myself at that last thought. Pictures of her delicate limbs entangled with mine are vivid and arousing...yet foreign. The object of my yearning is black. *They're different from us, right?*

In all my years of medical school, we only studied the negroid once, and it wasn't pleasant. It's not that I ever agreed with the theories, there was nothing proven to be scientifically different, but I still didn't know any better. My contact with them had been very slim outside of music and movies, even in my travels...but I want her. I will not deny that my body and mind are reacting to her like they've never reacted to any other woman before; nothing close to this.

"You know it's natural right?" Rolf whispers in my ear, "the desire to fuck a woman any way God made her. Height, weight...*color.*" I lick my lips, still watching her. "Only *they* tell you it's not."

"And who the fuck are they," I growl, looking Rolf dead on. His eyes light up as he takes a deep pull from his cigarette, holding in the smoke. With a grin he exhales slowly, letting out a steady stream of rolling white fog.

"My dear boy, *they* are the ones who are too puerile to

wrap their minds around a natural attraction to a succulent creature like that," he points his cigarette in her direction and I feel a small twinge of jealousy knowing my friend has also noticed her beauty, "*They* secretly desire to make love to her, but they won't because they lapped up ignorance from the time they were at their mutter's teet. Their communal minds won't let them stray through...enticing gardens. So, *they* poison the rest of us, and say 'if *they* can't have them, no one should'."

A waiter in white brocade linen with a red and black fez approaches our table, "Herr Bliss," he addresses Rolf quietly, bending down and stretching out his hand, balancing a small silver platter with a note resting atop.

"Shokran," Rolf nods to him while opening the note. I can tell by his silence that something is wrong.

"What is it?" I ask, still not taking my eyes from her.

"We return home tomorrow, early...pack tonight."

The crowd begins to applaud as her song is over, I stand to my feet clapping loudly shouting a "BRAVO!" It catches her attention for a brief moment, my heart almost stops when our eyes meet. She gives me a petite coy smile, but it soon leaves her face when she looks down toward Lottie and Dottie. They both shoot disapproving looks between us, but I don't care. I make my way to the stage, but I'm too late.

She departs behind the heavy curtain, just as two burly men hold out their hands to escort me away from her direction. A growl curls up through my throat from deep inside my chest. I ball my fists ready to tear through them to get to her. I step forward to the biggest one first with a smile on my face, but suddenly Rolf's hand is around my arm pulling me back.

"Now-now...temper-temper...we must mind your hands *surgeon*. No more boxing gloves for you, remember?"

He's right. Long since becoming a surgeon, I had put my

boxing days behind me. My hands were my art then, and most definitely now, however, the temper never left. My quick ire was the very reason I began boxing--to release the anger I had for my father on any poor, credulous soul that dared enter my ring. I count backward from ten, un-ball my fists, and try to look around the two giant walls of flesh to see where she had gone. *My Angel.* Again, Rolf is pulling me.

"Come. We must go, our return to Vienna is urgent." I shake my head 'no'. "Emil, I have seen her here before. Once we discover why our Vater's have summoned us and we evade their wishes like we always do, we will return. You for her, and me for—"

I spin around to him wild-eyed, searching his face, curiously desperate to learn what he is about to tell me, but he just smiles, that same smile I've been seeing for the past month. He slaps my back and guides me toward the exit, but I continue to look back over my shoulder; searching for her.

"Come," Rolf chuckles, "let us get our breasty guests home."

4

DADDY DEAREST

In a family manor on a hill
In a cavernous den
A man has struck a deal with the devil

VIENNA | NOVEMBER 1939

Emil

"**M**ein Gott, Vater, was hast du getan!?" [*My God, Father, what have you done!?*] I had only been home an hour after arriving in Vienna from Marrakech when my father commanded my presence at our family home, sending a car around for me to ensure my swift arrival. The heat from the large fireplace in his study engulfs my face with flames as I look at the stamped papers in my hands. My name has been forged by my father's pen, confirming my place in the Third Reich as a military surgeon. I can feel the hairs on the back of my neck peak from the smug grin on his face. He stands behind me, proud of what he has done. This is no doubt another power play—a venture of financial gain. Using me as a pawn like he has done in the past while dangling the security of my future in front of me.

I should have known there was something devious happening when Rolf cut our time short in Marrakech, after receiving a letter from his father summoning us both back to Vienna at once. We have long known that our fathers are depthless, money-hungry warmongers; the first to welcome Anschluss, happy to attune themselves with any creeping, crawling thing that increases their position and pockets. The only difference between our fathers is my family's wealth comes from old money. My mother's Austrian side is deeply seeded in the bohemian aristocracy, but Rolf's family, on the other hand, wreaks of Neureich.

Rolf's father capitalized off of the 1st World War, bringing a quiet shame on Rolf's head; a shame my friend has carried about his neck like an albatross. Though he is often loved for his money and good looks, he is ever on the fringe of society. Never fully being accepted into the fold because of his father's ways, and the proximity of their wealth. As if one's family being rich for over 200 years is any better or worse than one's family being rich for only 20—money is money.

Neither of our fathers have had more than two words to say to us in person, but always manage to be disappointed no matter how hard either of us try to impress them. Rolf gave up trying long ago, using his father's money and influence to travel the world, collecting art and artifacts, while I became a surgeon. It is thrice now that my father has pushed out the age on my trust fund claiming that my small excursions and chosen profession were "immature" and "not in line" with his desired path for my life. *I'm a fucking surgeon.* Most normal fathers would be proud to have a son that holds life in his hands, but not my father. The family business, the connections, the dealings, and hands changing money is what he wants for me—and will stop at nothing to get.

It was my father's need to control every aspect of my life that pushed me into boxing, then into being a doctor. If it weren't for my mother, I'd have been successful at neither, and I would be as greasy as he is today. My mother often interceded when it came to the relationship between father and I. Though he hated how she doted on me, he seldom denied her. I didn't know if it was because of his love for her or because the business he ran essentially belonged to her family, and she controlled the majority shares. It was her only dominance over him.

"You begin tomorrow." He pours himself a Port and rolls it around in his mouth, closing his eyes at the sweetness of both its taste and the victory of once again interfering in my life.

"...no, I won't do this. This whole war is wrong...that bastard is wrong! I won't—"

Snarling, glinting teeth are in my face before I complete my protest.

"You will do exactly what I tell you to do! The papers are already signed! Do you not understand that we are one of the five wealthiest families in Vienna? The only reason you breathe is because my money shields your ideals! The Führer will know that this family is loyal! I will not have you traipsing about, shirking your responsibility to me and your mutter!"

I wipe the spittle from my face in silent protest.

"What about my patients?"

My father backs away from me, waving his hand in disgust.

"What about them? You will have plenty more patients to fill their spots, patients worthy of your skill."

I lunge at my father, gripping my hands in his lapel so tightly my knuckles pale. He struggles against my steel grasp. I am no longer the small child he was once able to prevail physically. He brings his hands up through my arms, wrapping his long fingers around my neck, pushing his thumbs against my larynx. I slam him against his desk, knocking a crystal paperweight to the floor. At the sound of the crash, his study doors burst open, and two SS storm their way to me, pulling my hands from his lapel, and yanking me backward until I almost stumble from my feet. The bastard had them waiting for me. He knew what my reaction would be to his 'request', my temper often going unchecked, but never on this level. Once I'm in their hands, I calm myself and watch as the old man gasps for breath between his gritted teeth.

"Just as I thought?" He pushes up from the desk, "Always too fucking sensitive." Without warning, the back of his hand, rings and all, flies through the air and draws swiftly across my face with a loud, powerful *thwack!* I don't give him the pleasure of seeing me wince. I don't even bring my hand to my jaw to relieve the acute, throbbing pain.

"You will do this," he snarls at me like a dog, sucking in air in malicious grunts through his nose, "You will all but bleed this family's patriotism if you care about your future and the well-being of your mutter!"

My eyes widen at the threat to my mother.

"No son, I would never lay a finger to her, but think what *will* happen. Where will she go if all the money, her homes, everything is gone? Do you want to see her on the streets? Begging, peddling herself to survive? More than likely I'll be dead, your wish come true...but where will she be, ja? She'll become the old whore of some fat general all because you refused to serve your country!"

Though I know his scenario is close to impossible, my heart can't bear the pain of seeing the woman who birthed me, the woman who protected me time and again from my father's caustic rants and demands, becoming anything close to what he just described. Witnessing my surrender, my father gives a slight nod to the soldiers. I feel their hands let go of my shoulders and arms.

"Your *improved* practice will begin here in Vienna. You're lucky, you already have a shingle, then the Führer has plans for you in Paris."

"Paris?"

"Yes. But when, I don't know. Ah, and your traveling papers will be returned to you then, and not before. We can't have you skipping around, now can we?" My father's grin is wide and mean, and one day I will knock it from his face. "Oh, and your friend, that Neureich trash," he snaps his fingers, trying to recall his name as if he hadn't seen him by my side practically every day since my childhood.

"Rolf. He is not *trash*. He is the best man I know."

"Yes, well, he'll be going to boot camp."

"WHAT!?" The soldiers move toward me, and my father chuckles.

"Don't worry my son. You'll see your friend again. His father was able to buy him a cushion position, so I've heard...maybe one day he'll join you in Paris" he shrugs.

My blood is on fire. Rolf sent to boot camp, and both of us pawned off to protect families we hate. Is this life? Not the life I planned. Yes, I knew the war was imminent, but Rolf and I had designs to stay away from it any way we could. Now here we were, sold into it by our fathers, to the ultimate bidder. No, this is not life.

5

HEADING HOME

On a particular day
In the city of Paris
Three blocks from a Metro

PARIS | JUNE 1940

Emil

R olf picks me up from my newly appointed surgery in a long black car that gleams in the daylight. I can see him sitting inside, his head leaning against the window while his driver sits stiffly in the front.

"Must you escort me to my new home in this God-forsaken car," I ask, rolling my eyes while opening the door.

"Ja, Herr Oberstarzt. Mein Vater zahlt nur für das Beste." [*Yeah, my Colonel. My father only pays for the best.*] Rolf retorts flatly, still looking out of the window.

Since his return from bootcamp, his mood has become more fretful and somber. His drinking is no longer relegated to parties or after 5 pm, but anytime during the day seems fine for him now, judging from the open flask in his hand. His smiles are rare. I have tried all I can to relieve him of his burdens, but I don't know what they are aside from this war and his parents. The man that sits next to me is an almost 180-degree about-face from the man that sat next to me in that pink lounge in Marrakech not but a few months ago. "Come, let us get you to your new home," he grumbles taking a swig from his flask, "your father doesn't want so many city distractions for you here," he wags his finger at me mockingly.

While Rolf's father had no problems with him living in a sprawling apartment within the city limits, my father had strict instructions for me. He insisted I move into a small manor home on the outskirts of the city on the rim of a small village to ensure my isolation. I have my suspicions that a large part of this command was due to my mother, her own limited efforts to keep me out of the city, away from harm and out of trouble. I doubt my father cared either way, but the directive was still handed down from him. I was to make my own way and hire my own staff; while living alone and traveling into the city every day for my patients which currently consisted of almost no one having just moved to Paris several days ago, right after Rolf.

"Your car will arrive tomorrow so you won't have to worry about riding around in this machine," Rolf swipes his hand around languidly in a circle, his mouth turning up at the sides; a tiny smile that doesn't quite reach his eyes.

I sigh at my friend, then sit back, ready to see this home my father has acquired for me, no doubt stolen from some poor family. I force the thought to the back of my mind, scrunching my eyes and bringing my finger to my lips to stop myself from vomiting. I open my eyes to the sound of

Rolf knocking on the clear window partition separating us from his driver, an elderly French Jewish man that Rolf insisted on having as his chauffeur and majordomo. Rolf made certain his family was well taken care of, best he could, and that his man had two sets of papers, one to carry on his person while out in the street carrying out Rolf's small errands and another in the car glove compartment just in case, leaving absolutely nothing to chance. We pull off, beginning our journey to my dwelling. We ride down the streets in silence. I'm trying to think of anything but where I'm being escorted while Rolf is lost in his own thoughts. The driver makes a right at a corner adjacent to a Metro station, and it is Rolf who spots her first, shifting in his seat he points to the window.

"Emil, look...isn't that *her*?" he taps the window and I lazily look over,

"Her, who?"

"The girl. The one from the lounge in Marrakech," he taps the partition and asks the driver to slow down.

"Why on earth would she be here," I scoff looking out my own window, "It's not her...she'd be crazy to be here."

Rolf chuckles, "Beauty has never been a testament for brains my friend. I'm telling you, it's her—come look."

I roll my eyes and scoot over, squinting to get a better look. There are several soldiers in my line of sight, but when one of them steps aside, I'm afforded a clear view directly into their huddle and realize it *is* her, screaming and kicking as her clothes are being ripped from her torso. A rush of heat surges through my body and a familiar red veil lowers itself over my head.

"HALT!"

Rolf, without a second thought to my command, bangs on the partition, "Arrêtez-vous ici!" [*Stop here!*]

At Rolf's command, his man pulls over abruptly and parks in front of the Metro.

I fling open the car door, my blood boiling, sending small pin pricks over my skin. My fists are clenched at my sides and my long strides carry me swiftly to the source of the commotion.

6

A LITTLE BOY WONDERS

Deep in the woods
Past a small village
On the outskirts of Paris

THE PARISIAN COUNTRYSIDE | MAY 1940

David

It is too dark and I can't see. I can hear Maman crying as Papa whispers to her that, "it will be alright," and that, "it is for the best". It is cool and I am hungry, but most of all I miss my teddy bear and my choo-choo train. Papa made me leave them behind, he said they were too much to carry. Maman shouted at him and he said I could take my teddy, but there was banging at the door and when PaPa grabbed me trying to leave my room quickly, he picked up the wrong bear. Maman is too sad now, so I don't want to complain.

How will my teddy sleep at night without me to hold

him? He will be sad and looking for me? How will I get a message to him that I am alright, and with Maman and Papa in the woods and he can come visit me? He would be scared to come alone. He would have to unlock our doors and cross the big street, pass the cars and the angry men in their grey jackets. Then he would have to wait in a smelly home with dirt floors and then walk through the woods at night all by himself. No! He can't make that trip, it would be too much for him. He should stay by my trains, in my room where it is warm, and he can play with my other toys so they won't get lonely...yes. It is too far.

"David!" Papa calls my name and bends to me snapping his fingers near my face, I can see his hands and face well because of the very big moon Papa was waiting for.

"Oui, Papa"

"David, I know you are thinking, you are my smart boy, but I must be sure you are thinking of the right things. Do you understand?" I nod my head slowly at Papa, I think I understand, but I know he will tell me, "David, where we are going will be our home now, it is deep in the woods, so you must pay attention to everything around you. Look about you in the night and the day...look at the moon and the stars, study them and they will tell you where you are. Look at the trees David, study them also...memorize them, burn them into your mind." Maman keeps sniffling.

"He is only a little boy Ascher, must you give him so much!"

Papa raises from his knee, "Lower your voice woman," he whispers loudly to her, and she cries again, but this time he hugs her like he used to do in our home. I look at them both and decide I won't make Maman and Papa afraid for me anymore, so I hug Papa's leg tight to get his attention.

"Papa, I will learn, I promise."

He bends down to me again, holding Maman's hand, "Oui! Bon mon gosse [*Yes! Good my boy*]...I know you are little in stature, but now is the time to grow in your spirit and become a man, which means you must listen to everything around you. You must listen and mind me and your Maman every time, without fail, no matter how silly our game...every sound, every smell, every viewpoint, you must now make *them* your friends, do you understand David?"

"Yes, Papa."

He tousles my hair expecting me to giggle as always, but that is for little boys. I place my hand on his shoulder with a great clap, this is what I see my Grand-père do to my Papa when they part ways after a long visit, and my Papa always smiles...just like he does now.

"You make us proud David...now come, we must continue."

Maman takes my hand while we both follow Papa. I raise my head and sniff the air, then wave '*hello*' to a tall tree.

7

THE METRO

PART TWO

Surrounded by soldiers
On a street in Paris
Across from the Metro

PARIS | JUNE 1940

Victoire

My eyes blur and the Metro, my salvation, is no longer in view. There are only large moving globs that surround me. Hands upon hands tug at me. I can feel my skirt tearing at my waist. I don't know what I have done, I don't understand why they are stripping me, I can only go within myself, knowing this is the end. My dignity is lost, my life next? I have nothing to live for. I have lost my friends, my home, my parents, whatever is to come next, I will embrace it.

I. Just. Let. Go.

...until I see a pair of the most beautiful ocean blue eyes meet my own.

Emil

I CLOSE the gap between myself and the soldiers. They hover over her like bees. The one who is laughing the most and the loudest is the one I hone in on, the one who will bear the full weight of my fist. Rolf is on my heels, prepared to stop me from using my hands, but I won't let another one of these scheißkerle [*fucks*] touch her. The soldier sees me treading towards him and tosses my Angel from his hands. My ears ring hot with the sound of her fragile flesh and bones hitting the ground; a small cry of pain escapes her lips. Just as he is about to salute, I halt his pissy greeting with my left hand wrapped around his neck, holding him in place as I jab him twice in the jaw with my right. All the laughing ceases. They see my decorations and begin to scatter like roaches, back to their posts and prior business before this harassment started. There are a few that continue to mill around, but Rolf quickly disperses them. He buys their silence with his weeks' worth of rations for Miette's, which they quickly take and walk away excited to have entertainment and free meals that actually include real butter and salt.

"Wer sind Sie? Was ist Ihr Problem!?" [*Who are you? What is your problem!?*] the offending soldier croaks, gasping for breath. His wide eyes search me as he lifts his hand, flush against his jaw. Blood from his mouth oozes, dripping down slowly, creating small dark spots on the cuff of my uniform.

I answer him cooly. "Who am I? I am your fucking superior. Do you not know how to do your job properly?" My face is wild with madness, my hand still wrapped tightly around his neck.

Rolf taps my shoulder from behind, "You are causing a scene, Emil. We must go."

"I'm not finished with this piece of shite."

"Then hurry the fuck up, you've drawn attention from those officers down the street and they're coming this way...FUCK!"

Rolf pushes his hair back with his fingers and strolls over to the officers, his arms stretched wide, shrugging his shoulders.

I look down at her, "Es-tu blessée?" [*Are you hurt?*] my voice is flat and harsh, the rage inside me unwilling to soften. Her grim expression changes to shock at my question and her almond-shaped eyes stare at me in disbelief. I look up and see Rolf trying his best to stall the approach of the officers as their curiosity is piqued. I ask her again even more harshly, time is of the essence. "J'ai vous demandé si vous êtes blessée!" [*I said, are you hurt!*] she shakes her head swiftly from side to side, her eyes filled with tears. "Couvres-toi! Maintenant!" [*Cover yourself! Now!*] I can't bear the thought of other men looking at her, filling their eyes with a delight that should belong only to me. From the moment I saw her, the feeling of possession toiled within me. I watch as she begins pulling the tatters of her blouse closed with trembling fingers. Satisfied, I look to Rolf's driver across the street and whistle through my teeth, jerking my head signaling for him to bring the car around.

Tightening my grip on the soldier's neck I speak to her again, "Restez où vous êtes et nous vous aiderons. Ne parlez pas et regardez par terre, comprenez-vous?" [*Stay where you are, and we will help you. Do not speak, and keep your eyes to the ground, do you understand?*] she nods to me again. Her entire body now shakes with fear as she lowers her gaze to the ground. My heart squeezes at the thought that she fears me, fears for her life, I would never hurt her but she doesn't know this. Right now I can't let my mind linger on her emotions, I must finish with this problem in front of me or things for her could get much worse.

Victoire

I WIPE the small gravely rocks from my palms and wince at the pain in my knees. The soldier threw me down to the sidewalk hard, when he saw the stranger with the ocean blue eyes striding his way with the speed of the devil. I dab, absent-mindedly at the small specs of blood on my knees with my skirt.

"Couvres-toi! Maintenant!"

In shock, I look up at the stranger, trying to understand if he had just spoken to me in French...*of course he did*. My eyes take in his tall blonde frame and plump pink lips pulled tight over his gritted teeth. The soldier who pulled my hair and threw me down is in his grasp, his face turning shades of green and purple. I tremble in fear of his command, but it's an awkward fear. I don't feel that he has come to harm me, but his tone and presence command my respect. The way his eyes roll over my body, there is a pity there, and something else I can't put a finger on, and that is what causes me to tremble. He looks as if he wishes to sink his teeth into my flesh...but with or without malice, I cannot know. I don't lower my eyes from his as my fingers fumble to pull what is left of my blouse over my torn camisole. I only now notice it is barely covering my breast. For a moment, right before I pull the tatters over my skin, his eyes soften and I turn away.

He snarls at me, commanding my attention again as if my shyness offends him.

"Restez où vous êtes et nous vous aiderons. Ne parlez pas et regardez par terre, comprenez-vous?"

I nod to him afraid to speak. My entire body shaking with fear as I hear more footsteps approaching, I do as he says and lower my eyes to the ground.

Emil

MY RIGHT HAND IS POUNDING, *shit*, and the officers grow closer still. I quickly turn back to the soldier in my grasp, who so obviously does not speak French, and I bend to his ear so only he can hear me.

"I should rip out your fucking eyes with your own hands and shove them down your throat for looking at her and touching her, however, I will spare you Genosse. But should I ever see your piece of shite face again, I'll finish you off, where you stand, without a second thought, verstanden!?" I remove my hand from his throat, and he stumbles back landing on his rear. I lift him to his feet and straighten his uniform as the officers are now upon us.

I smile just as brightly as Rolf, stepping in front of my Angel with the pecan skin, hoping they don't look down, but it's a hard hope.

"Ah, schönen Tag," I click my heels and nod deeply. They both look me over with questioning smiles. Rolf steps back next to me, taking my lead in shielding her as the car pulls up by my side.

"Is there a problem, Oberstarzt," one of the officers asks while squinting his eyes to look at my name patch, "Ah, Oberstrazt von Konig, you are the new surgeon, ja?" I smile and click my heels again, removing my hat and placing it under my arm.

"At your service."

I shake his hand, while the other officer looks at the soldier who is still holding his jaw and then to the pecan skinned woman on the ground behind us. I smile again, tracing his line of sight.

Rolf catches my glance then clears his throat, "Hreggh, hmm. We had a small issue with this one is all. My friend here had chosen her to be a maid in his new home and she protested, but after some convincing, as you see, we are certain she will succumb to his request." My muscles are coiled and tight, ready to pounce should either one of them make a move toward her, the red veil is still upon me. The soldier who I jabbed twice, is about to say something through his cracked and bruised jaw, but I peer at him clenching my teeth, taking a small step forward to warn him not to cross me. His eyes lower to regard my closed fist and immediately he straightens his back saluting us and the two officers. He walks off towards the great mass of people standing against the wall, yelling as best as he can for them to form a line.

"Are you sure you want such an unruly woman taking care of your home, and black no less. How can she be trusted?"

I smile again and nod. "Well, as I am just moving in, what I have currently is of little to no value, most of my belongings are still being shipped, and if there is a problem, I will know who to blame." I thank God in heaven that she shows no indication of comprehending German, I don't know if she'd understand what Rolf and I are trying to do. Our fellow officers are unimpressed with my answer, but just as the curious one begins to speak again a woman's high-pitched voice calls from behind us. I turn to see a tall buxom blonde waving a handkerchief motioning for the two officers to come over. She points down at her companion a giggling brunette, and my gaze returns to the officers who now look like two hungry wolves that have been starved for months. I take this as my opportunity.

"Ah, let us not keep you from such charms. Paris holds many, many wonders." I arch my eyebrows with a lascivious grin. They nod in agreement and move on. As soon as they are down the sidewalk Rolf makes haste to open the car door, and I scoop the pecan-skinned Angel off the ground, into my arms. She feels so good, soft and warm, her trembling increases the rage in me, but the light scent of her perfume eases it quickly, turning it to desire and I force myself to think of every awful thing that I can to keep from growing hard.

I sit her in the seat between Rolf and me as he quietly speaks with the driver. For some reason, be it nerves or fear of discovery, I don't look her in the eye, or even turn my head in her direction. I set my sights on the road in front of us as the car pulls off.

"Quel est votre nom?" [*What is your name?*] I ask, keeping my voice low and calm, still focusing on the road ahead.

"Victoire. You speak French?" she whispers softly.

"Oui"

"...and your friend?"

Rolf gives her his best wolfish grin before answering her question, "Oui, Fräulein, je parle français." [*Yes, Miss, I speak French.*] Her head lowers to her skirt as she pulls it down, trying to reclaim a morsel of her dignity and bracing herself to ask her next question.

"Are you going to hurt me?"

"Non.

8

BACK TO MAMAN

Sifting through pictures
On a little settee
In a big house

CALIFORNIA | 1980

Lily

My eyes are wide as my mother reaches for the soft chenille blanket on the back of the settee, wrapping it around her shoulders, though it's 90 degrees outside.

"Maman, I never knew that happened to you!" I scoot closer and rub her arms up and down trying to heat her up. She shrugs and smiles at me.

"I am not cold ma Petite. Just the thought of that day, what could have been, still chills me." My heart tugs as tears well up in my eyes.

"Oh, non, non, non. Tsk, tsk," she sucks her teeth, "I do

not tell you this to make you cry Cherie! Do not cry, I am here, I am alive," she sings, caressing my cheek. I do as she says and wipe my tears. I show my mother that I too can be strong like her. She looks at her watch and sucks her teeth again, "Hmm, where is that tea?"

"Maman," I interrupt, "is this why there are no pictures of Grand-mère and Grand-père?"

She nods slowly.

"Oui, Petite...anything that I would have had to show you or give you I lost that day. I never did return to the house until many, many years later. By then it had changed so many hands, there would have been nothing left," she looks at me sadly, but then gives me a sweet smile pointing at her heart, "but I remember them in here. And when I went back, I found Lisette again! She lost Jean-Marc in the war, so she came to stay with me. She survived by living with his family in the countryside, where they managed until liberation," she smiles. "Not all was lost." She takes my hands in hers and rubs them like kindling a fire. The light tinkling sound of her bracelets delight my ears and bring back childhood memories of when I played dress up in her room. She sighs heavily and looks back at the pictures between us.

"Where did you go after that day Maman, did they...he, hurt you?"

"That very day they escorted me to the doctor's home, where I was to become his maid. I tried to tell them that I had my own home, a cottage not but a few miles away, but they convinced me it wouldn't be safe to live there alone. They later had papers drawn up for me, that would allow me to travel back and forth from his home should I be stopped, a few of my belongings were brought to me from my cottage and I was given two maids uniforms, one formal and one informal. I was terrified! I had never done domestic work before. Not any of my own cooking or cleaning, nothing! What if I did it wrong, would I be sent away? All I knew was how to make honey cake, my father's personal favorite, everything else I would have to learn and learn quickly. He saved my life. And he seemed kind enough but still, I sensed a hardness that I didn't want to cross. For many, many days I trembled in fear each time he spoke to me, I did all I could not to provoke him."

"How did you make it work?"

"I kept my distance," she says with an arched brow, then she giggles, remembering something that tickles her, and my eyes widen in curiosity, "Would you believe I mustered the courage to ask him for a subscription to a French house-keeping magazine?" We both laugh falling over each other.

"...and what did he say?"

"Well of course he said 'yes' after I told him that if he wanted a dinner that didn't include the taste of smoke, he must order this magazine to help me!"

9

PETIT MAISON

A distance from the city
In the countryside
A manor comes into view

THE HOUSE OF HERR VON KONIG | JUNE 1940

Victoire

I keep my eyes down as the car rolls to a stop. My ears strain, listening to the crunching sound of rocks beneath the tires. I am afraid to look up, afraid to see where they have taken me. When I do finally peer through the window, I see that we have stopped in front of an inviting, cream stoned petit maison with a large oak front door and matching shutters on the many windows. The grounds are well-kept and lush green trimmed bushes line the round driveway and path to the front of the house. A large fountain sits proudly in the middle of the round, also surrounded by green bushes and large white roses that are so fragrant, when I exit the car, my feet take pause and I close my eyes savoring the scent. The warmth of the sun blankets my face and I think of Capri. The tiny jewel beaches with little blue & white umbrellas, my skin deepening in color from this very same sun, and for a moment I'm forgetting where I am. The moment is lost as quickly as it came as I feel a faint deprivation. The warm rays of the bright burning star are replaced by a somber, heavier warmth of a different kind. I continue to keep my eyes shut as my nostrils fill with a balmy, citrus scent that blends with the roses, like a potion, magical and lovely.

"It would be best for you to go inside and refresh yourself, Fraülein. Forgive my rudeness, but this home is new to me, and as Herr Bliss has outfitted it in my absence, I will allow him to show you to your quarters." His voice is dark and deep, yet soothing, like being immersed in warm water. None of the grit nor anger lingers from before, with his hand around the soldier's throat. *He is trying...open your eyes.* My eyelids flutter open, and once again I am met with the bluest oceans. My savior's looming height forces me to look up, where I regard his aquiline nose sitting a mere fingertip above soft pink, bow lips. An angular, yet granite jawline gives balance to his high cheekbones and, seemingly permanent, furrowed brows of gold. My arm resists a magnet-like pull to reach up and cup my hand over his cheek. He continues to stare into my eyes as if waiting for this physical acknowledgment of his presence, but I don't dare.

"Oui, Monsieur."

I lower my gaze to the ground and walk around him cautiously, immediately feeling his heat dissipate and for a brief moment, my body aches at the loss of his warmth. My eyes find Herr Bliss who smiles at me patiently, waving his hand for me to come and follow him, but before I take another step I turn on my heels to my savior with the eyes blue as the ocean. His back is to me, but at the sound of my return he cocks his ear, and his head turns partially over his shoulder.

"Monsieur, I--I must thank you for your kindness today, you and Herr Bliss, I owe you my life. I must be honest Monsieur, and tell you I have never paid attention to my maids before, and have acquired no knowledge of their work and ways, but in return for your graciousness I promise to you that I will do all I can to keep your home." I am returned a slight nod. "Monsieur, what is your name...wh--what shall I call you?" I ask, barely above a whisper, praying that it is okay for me to address him this way. He straightens his back, cracking his neck as his broad shoulders move up and down. His stroll to me is slow. My heart begins to pound with fear, fear that I have overstepped, that I have indeed mistaken his kindness. I recoil slightly as he walks past. Suddenly, I feel him take residence behind me and goosebumps form up my neck as he inhales, his aquiline nose only millimeters away. He says nothing for what seems like hours; I'm scared, and I ready myself to run. With another deep inhale at the nape of my neck, his voice is a whisper.

"My name is Emil— August— Odilo —Sigismund— von Konig...and you may call me Herr von Konig...for now."

I don't move, except to lower my gaze to the ground, offering him my nape, my urge to run turning into a pulsating fever between my legs. I hear him breathing, feel him examining me. He makes a final extravagant exhale that travels down my spine sending electrical currents that awaken all the delicate parts of my body and I cross my legs at the ankles involuntarily squeezing my thighs together. My eyes close for a brief moment at the tiny pleasure of his breath, hot against the back of my neck, and then he is gone, the crunching of the rocks underfoot indicating his retreat.

10

A LITTLE BOY MAKES A NEW FRIEND

At the edge of a wood
Behind a manor home
A little boy smiles

THE PARISIAN COUNTRYSIDE | OCTOBER 1940

David

Maman says I mustn't follow Papa and his friends. She says it is not safe for me, but I want to be a man like Papa has asked me. Sometimes, I follow behind them when they go to gather wood but when they leave carrying the big metal toys Maman says I am "not to play with", I go another way and I visit my new friend. I like her. She is kind to me. Sometimes, I wait for her at the edge of the woods and when the light comes on in the big window I wave to her. I stretch my arm big so she can see me and she waves back! On those days, if I wait a little bit she will put out some warm bread and milk for me, sometimes even jam. I take home what I haven't eaten to Maman even though I know I might get a hiding.

I never stay too long. I know I'm not supposed to leave the woods, Papa has warned me many times. My friend even left me a book; it has many pictures. I made a small hole in the ground in our new home. When Maman and Papa are not there I fetch it and look at the bright colors and animals. There is a girl near my home who is teaching me to read it, but mostly I like to look at the bears. They remind me of my Teddy and I hope he is okay. Maybe he was able to visit my new friend and tell her how much I like bread and jam and books, I bet he did! He can't find me so far away in the woods, so he spoke to my friend! I'm so happy he got to meet her!

11

GHOSTS

On an early morning
In the warm kitchen
Of a quiet house

THE HOME OF HERR VON KONIG | OCTOBER 1940

Victoire

I am alone in this house. The greying rooms all whisper of my abandonment. Defiantly, I visit them every day giving them a sweep of a dust cloth, and fluff of a pillow. My only solace is the scarce company of a strange little boy who stands at the edge of the woods behind the house across from the chicken coops and garden. Early in the mornings, every so often, he stands next to one of the big, knotted trees awaiting my arrival to the kitchen which harbors a large window above the sink facing the wood. I can see him before he sees me, so I turn on the light to indicate my presence. Once I come into his view, he waves his little arms as big as he can and I wave back just as happily. Why a little boy is in the woods alone, I don't know, but I have my suspicions.

He's like a little wild rabbit, running away if I get too close; I've tried. A few times I've taken slow steps toward him, but in a flash, he turns and disappears deep into the woods, not to return until another odd morning. I've come to think of it as a little game we play. I saw him for the first time a few months ago while plucking eggs in the coop. He watched me intently for a little while and I waited to see if there was anyone to come and fetch him. Not seeing any danger, I smiled and waved. From that day forward, he has become my little spot of company in this lonely place. My little friend is here again today. So, I heat up some bread in the oven, pour some fresh milk into an empty bottle and wrap a few strong lashings of blackberry jam into brown wax paper. I set it all out on the back steps for my little wild rabbit then go about my work, happy to see him well with the knowledge that his tiny belly will be full for the long morning ahead. Once I close the door, I am again left with my loneliness. I think of my mother and father, wondering if they ever found my cottage or if they too were rounded up and taken away. Tears sting my eyes as I remember the last time I spoke to them, shouting for them to choose reason. When they would not, I left. I continue to move about the rooms dusting and straightening. Before I know it, the clock strikes 3p.m. and it is time for me to begin preparing Herr von Konig's supper.

I enjoy this time of day. Preparing his supper turns my focus to something other than my parents or the life I led before my capture. It gives me purpose as I near the end of a long day alone. A small part of me enjoys the idea of cooking for him, though I know I shouldn't, I do. There is another part of me that wishes he would be here along with me during the days, his brooding aura moving about the house quietly, leaving behind only subtle indications of his presence...a cigar ash perhaps, the faraway tinkling of ice in a whisky glass, a pair of shoes out of place. A specter keeping me company. The thought of his ocean blue eyes and the scent of bergamot sends tingles to my lower belly and soon I feel the dew of my desire slick between my legs. I shake my head clear and concentrate on what I am making for his supper. I watch the carrots, celery and a few small potatoes roll back and forth as I mindlessly stir. The perfume of spices permeates the house giving a small semblance of life to the darkening corridors.

I promised Herr von Konig my best, and I intend to keep my promise as I bring the spoon to my lips, blowing a light stream of cool air over the brown liquid. I sip it carefully and the flavor is robust—I am pleased...he will be pleased. I want to please him. I turn the pot very low, spooning a portion out for myself. While I let my serving cool, I go about setting the table preparing for Herr von Konig's arrival. I lay out a spoon for his stew, a knife to sweep butter over his bread and a white napkin to dab the corners of his perfect mouth. The clock chimes 7 p.m. He will be here any moment, weary from the day and hungry. I greet him every night. Once he enters the door and I hang his coat, I serve him, wait for him to taste his food, and be dismissed. He releases me, always with the same simple three words. He says them to me as if he is praying.

Emil

"THANK YOU, VICTOIRE." I watch her through my lashes as she gives me an almost imperceptible nod before leaving my presence. As the stew before me cools, my mind wanders. My father continues his campaign, writing letters to express the importance of my making good inroads with my fellow officers. That I must "attend their parties", "uphold the von Konig name" and show my face whenever possible, as if being one of three resident military surgeons in all of Paris isn't enough— *bastard*. Between my father's demands for my social upkeep, the surgery, which is now seeing more patients by the day and Rolf's continued, doleful withdrawal into himself, all I desire is to concentrate on the ghost which haunts my home. Since the day Victoire stepped across my threshold she has kept her promise of doing all she can to make sure that I have, what one would call, the comforts of home.

She has even gone so far as to practically demand I order her magazines and catalogs to teach her how to keep a tidy house and cook hot meals. She trembled that day when she came to me to ask for assistance. Her voice was strong, but her eyes were low. How could I resist such a creature, asking for help to ensure that I am pleased with her? Every morning there is strong coffee, eggs and toast, meats and cheese are wrapped delicately in brown wax paper with a white string and lain beside my plate for me to take for lunch. And every night my dinner is prepared and served to me by a solemn-faced paragon of femininity. Just as soon as she appears from her hideaway in the kitchen to serve me, she is gone, not to be seen again until the next evening. I am left with a hot meal, the faint smell of cinnamon and roses and an ache in my chest. How I wish to see the coy smile she gave me that night I saw her on stage in Marrakech. I often wonder if she remembers me, but I haven't the courage to speak to her beyond my three words to her every night, "Thank you, Victoire," in which I hope I am able to convey my deepest appreciation of her efforts, and my even deeper desire to know her.

It is with that final rumination that I pick up my bowl and head to the kitchen to find my ghost.

The faint sound of music drifts through the kitchen door as I push it open gently with my shoulder.

"Herr von Konig!"

Victoire raises from her seat at the small wooden kitchen table with a start, her eyes wide, mouth agape and her hands wringing in her apron.

"Is something wrong? Is it the music? It is German, I promi—"

I raise my hand to cut her off as I give her a slight smile, but it is the hand that holds the napkin keeping a barrier between my fingers and the hot bowl of stew. Within seconds the searing pain moves through my fingers and I drop the bowl to the ground shattering it, splattering her stew across the floor. I grab my hand, gritting my teeth. I have an operation in three days, my hands must be perfect.

"Merde!," she gasps, grabbing a towel from the sink and running it under what I presume to be cold water. "Sit Monsieur, sit!" She rushes to me and takes my hand pressing the cool cloth into my fingers soothing the heat that dances about them. "Keep holding this to your fingers."

Her touch is light and her hands are soft. On instinct, she kneels in front of me and caresses my cheek softly. Once she realizes what she's done she retreats, casting her eyes low. She removes her apron and commences to wipe up the soup and shards of the porcelain bowl that I so clumsily dropped.

I start towards the floor, "Please, let me help you."

She looks up to me in shock, her dark brown eyes searching my face.

"Non, please–your hand." She pushes the final drops of the stew up into the apron, walks over to the rubbish bin and dumps everything inside: soup, bowl shards and apron, giving an exasperated look. "I am sorry Monsieur, but I will have to ask you for another apron." I stare at her apron-less figure now that the oversized white piece of material is gone, and I am given an unobstructed view of her body. The black gown cutting a curvaceous figure against the cream of the kitchen walls. Her breasts are full and high, and the white stitched darts in the front of her uniform lead down to her narrow waist. I feel myself stiffen at the thought of wrapping my hands around her and pulling her down to me, right here, where I sit on this chair. Feeling her ample ass, so soft and supple on my lap. Her legs spread astride me. Her heat, along with the aroma of her arousal pulling me to her...

"Herr von Konig?" The sound of my name snaps me back from my thoughts.

"Yes?"

"The apron?" she questions as she looks at me inquisitively. I nod to her.

"Yes, I shall order you a new one in the morning and bring it home tomorrow evening."

Another inquisitive look.

"You will be gone tomorrow? But it is Saturday...your day o–," she stops herself and begins to study her shoes. "Thank you, Herr von Konig. I will make do until Sunday morning." We remain in awkward silence for a while.

"Please, sit. Your supper is getting cold," I gesture toward her seat. She looks at me with a slight sparkle in her eye that turns to worry once she remembers my hand.

"Monsieur, we must first replace your towel and then I will make you another bowl."

"Of course," I retort flatly, admiring her graceful movements as she glides toward me to fetch the warmed cloth. She runs the cloth under cool water and re-applies it gently to my fingers, then plucks another bowl from the cupboard and ladles out a hearty helping of stew sitting it before me. Victoire continues to stand, and I realize she is waiting for our ritual. I bring a spoonful to my lips, never taking my eyes from her. "Thank You, Victoire."

Though her head is down, I see her eyes flutter and I catch the hint of a small coy smile, the one I have been waiting months to see again.

Victoire

HE WATCHES ME. When I bring the spoon to my lips, he watches me. When I lick my lips catching the liquid that escapes my mouth, he watches me. His ocean blue eyes darken like a storm. He lights a small thin cigar and crosses his legs, his ankle at his knee, the burning of his fingers forgotten, and he watches me.

"Herr von Konig?"

"Yes," he purses his pink, bow lips, bringing the cigar between them, puffing in gently. His cheeks hollow ever so slightly before he blows the sweet-smelling smoke from the side of his mouth. I am mesmerized by the tiny flick of his tongue across his bottom lip, "Your question?" His deep, husky tone interrupts my thoughts. He raises his golden eyebrows quizzically awaiting my response.

I take in a deep breath.

"Where did you learn French, if you don't mind my

asking? Your accent is exceptionally good?" He smirks at me, his eyes still watching. He puffs his cigar again, this time blowing the smoke from his nostrils with a strong sigh. "Forgive me if I have overstepped. I didn't mean to be too familiar."

His eyes search mine and his brows furrow.

"You really must stop apologizing," he says quietly but sternly, "It doesn't suit you." I drop my spoon and stare back at him, straight in the eyes. He's right. I only apologize because I fear for my life, but everything in me says this is not something I need to do. "Bon."

Another smirk. This one calls for the dew to return between my legs. I cross my ankles and squeeze my thighs together hoping to stop the pulsing sensations. I lick my lips and watch his eyes flicker quickly to my mouth then back to my eyes. Again, we stare at each other, again his answer is delayed.

I work up my nerve again, "Your French, mein Herr?"

"My mother," he pauses, flicking ash into a small cup I set out for him, "she is of French extraction, as well as Austrian. There were many summers I was sent to visit her sisters, here in Paris, when I was a small child."

"Besides German and French, do you speak any other languages?"

"Oui. Anglais."

I smile broadly, forgetting myself, rushing into speaking English.

"I speak English too!"

He chuckles while snuffing out his cigar, the sweet smokey scent wafting away slowly.

"Interesting, and who taught you?" he asks with a straight face but a sparkle in his eyes that excites me more, the weight of his presence lifting just a bit.

"Both of my parents are American, Creole and Haitian from New Orleans!" And just like that, my happiness at finding commonality with Herr von Konig is dashed at the thought of my parents. My heart pounds in my chest with anxiety and tears sting the back of my eyes. I lower my head and let a single set of tears fall silently, then reigning in my emotions I jump up from the table and begin to clear its contents. I stand silently at the sink, heartbroken, immobile, unable to return to our exchange, and the silence is deafening. Once the last bowl is clean I hear his chair move back from the table, and like that day in front of the fragrant roses a few months ago I feel him behind me, his heat radiating through me, warming my blood.

"I am sorry about your parents," he whispers softly. His breath at the back of my neck again, sending luscious shivers down my spine. I fight this feeling, shaking my head vigorously back and forth while moving toward the door. Before I make it past the kitchen threshold, into the dark corridor I feel his hand wrap around my wrist. The action is gentle, sending tiny electric sparks up my arm, through my shoulder, down to my heaving breasts awaking my nipples. My mind is a soup of arousal and sadness. I don't look back, I only wait, holding my breath as his thumb traces a slow delicate line, burning me from my wrist to my fingertips, where he then let's go.

"Thank you, Victoire."

I nod my head and rush through the door.

INTELLIGENCE

Riding down the road
In a long black car
In the city

PARIS | NOVEMBER 1940

Emil

I'm in Rolf's car again, as we make our way through the grey Paris streets. I can almost hear his gears and wheels turning as he thinks silently. Over these past few months, my friend has withdrawn even more. The bright smile and playful manner I once witnessed, not but a year ago, is now a muddle of grunts and a distant gaze that cuts through me and everyone around him. I turn and study him closer. His skin is pale, and a darkness has set in under his eyes, he twists and rubs his pinky finger constantly, like a nervous twitch...I make conversation.

"How is your mother?" Rolf's head is against the window as he looks out longingly, "Rolf?"

"Hm?" Another grunt.

"Your mother, how is she?" My eyebrows move upward slowly as I wait for an intelligible response. He clears his throat, removing his head from the glass, looking straight ahead and reaching in his pocket for his flask.

"Mother is fine. Whining, as always, about my boredom with her stories of her knitting club, and on my case about my 'consistent disinterest' in the comings and goings of Dottie Schneagle." I smirk and chuckle remembering the last time we saw the Schneagle twins after dropping them at their hotel room. Lottie practically had her hands down my pants, with her Triple D breasts pressed firmly against my dinner jacket trying her best to arouse me, but there was no chance after I had seen the object of my desire on stage that night, Victoire. Dottie, however, had the face of a prune, all puckered up and red from Rolf's tactless, brutal rebuff.

"Ah, yes. Die Zwillingstitten," [*The twin titties*] I croon.

Rolf laughs for the first time in almost forever, since that night when he came bounding into the pink lounge. I want to know what has happened to my friend, so I ask, "Was belastet dich, Rolf, du bist nicht du selbst? Kann ich dir helfen...du weißt, dass du mir alles erzählen kannst?" [*What has been bothering you Rolf, you're not yourself? Can I help you...you know you can tell me anything?*] He snaps his head around to me, his eyes searching mine, trying to look for an answer I'm not sure whether or not I'm able to give, but for my friend, I will try.

"Herr Bliss, we have arrived," his driver calls, parking the car on the curb next to the intelligence building. Rolf turns from me to address his driver.

"Thank you," he replies to the portly, salt and pepper haired man, "My dear friend, have my driver take you anywhere you wish to go," he gives me a mischievous grin reminiscent of the old Rolf. "I'm sure you'll do the obvious and make your way to that pretty little maid you keep hold up in that stone prison that passes for a home." I feel heat lowering over my ears, an evident physical response to his teasing, a mix of embarrassment and anger. Rolf slaps his hand on my shoulder, "We'll revisit your questions another time, ja? You should cover your ears, Emil," he chuckles shaking his head, "...and remember that we are to attend the officer's dinner tomorrow night!"

My eyes grow wide as he exits the car, striding swiftly around the front to my side. *Another fucking dinner.* More and more of my weekends have been spent rubbing elbows with filth. These dinners and parties are nothing more than the scum of the earth displaying their gratuitous, ill-gotten wealth. The nights often spill over into the next day. Most times I stay overnight in my surgery not wanting to make the trek home, then I awake, feeling guilty for leaving Victoire home alone. However, I must admit to myself that I am comforted when she is there to meet me when I walk through the door the next morning. She awaits me with her skin glowing in the morning light, a brilliant pecan color of perfection, her kind eyes giving me a brief shy smile before humbly looking at the floor as she greets me and takes my coat. On such mornings she indulges me with a slice of her honey cake, topped with sweet cream and drizzled honey and a strong cup of coffee. The smell of the cake warm from the oven mixed with her scent of cinnamon and roses waters my mouth. When I lick the last of the cream and honey from my spoon, I imagine that my tongue is tasting her...lapping at the sweet essence between her thighs.

Suddenly, my mouth is dry, and I almost forget my friend. Rolf whistles and snaps his fingers next to my ear.

"Another fucking dinner, Rolf!" I growl, my jaw tight and teeth grinding. His lips curl upward at my reaction, a shell of a smile.

"Tsk, Tsk, our father's orders remember." He bows sarcastically, then straightens himself to tap the top of the car emphasizing his command, "See you tomorrow at eight my friend," he says as he turns and makes his way toward the building.

I stick my head out of the window and look up at the edifice which reads, in freshly painted letters,

ADMINISTRATION

which is code for, Intelligence.

"Administration!?" I shout to Rolf raising my brow high. He turns to face me while walking backward slowly.

"Something new...Vater's connections! Friday, 8 o'clock!" he shouts, then turns on his heel practically bumping into a stern-looking officer who clicks his heels and salutes. Rolf stands stiff, hesitating for a moment. I turn my head quickly and tell the driver to press on, I don't want to see Rolf's return salutation.

13

BREAKFAST

In a bed
In a very cold room
Waking up for a busy morning

THE HOME OF HERR VON KONIG | NOVEMBER
1940

Victoire

My eyes roll under my lids following my mind's train of thought. *Herr von Konig has a surgery today. He will be up early, I must get his breakfast.* I blink open my heavy lids and rub my hands up and down my arms vigorously, warming myself before sitting up on the edge of my bed. I'm still in my thoughts when my feet touch the cold wooden floor. Days have passed since the night Herr von Konig joined me for supper. The echoes of our conversation play like a melody to me, and I wonder why I didn't say more, stay longer, then I remember...*my parents*.

I shiver and rub my arms again, looking around for my housecoat. The nights and early mornings grow colder, and my quarters are not immune to the chill. The many blankets piled on my bed do their job for the most part, but my thoughts and dreams of Herr von Konig do more than enough to keep my body warm. The memory of his hand around my wrist still lights a small flame inside me, one that I don't want to go out. It swaddles me when I know he himself will not. Finally, spotting my housecoat, I wrap it tightly around my body and tiptoe from my room to the toilet in haste to complete my morning ablutions and begin yet another lonely day. Perhaps the little boy will be waiting for me today? I giggle at the thought of my little wild rabbit waving to me happily from his tree.

At a quarter to six, I make my way down the stairs to prepare breakfast, serenely moving about the kitchen, keeping a sharp lookout for my little friend. I place two boiled eggs in cozies to keep them warm, and a few slices of toast in an ornate silver rack. I wrap up some cured meats and cheese in brown wax paper and tie it with white string for Herr von Konig's lunch. *He will be very hungry,* I think to myself. I unwrap the paper and add a few slices of bread. I look at the clock again, *7 am*, and no sight of my little friend, I sigh in disappointment, *he will not be here today.* My heart sinks, but I wish him well on whatever journey the day takes him.

I move swiftly to the dining room laying out Herr von Konig's paper, a plate, napkin, fork, knife, butter and his favorite, marmalade. I gently set down a coffee cup then tuck the wax paper package closely under his plate. I hear his footsteps above and hurry back to the kitchen. I know I will have just enough time to set everything out so his food remains warm before he makes it to the dining room. I remove the eggs from their cozies and place them in tiny silver egg cups, then set everything on a serving tray, including a small coffee service. I return quickly to the dining room and sit his eggs and toast on the table, pour his coffee and make my way back to the kitchen before his footsteps hit the bottom of the stairs, and there I remain until I hear the tinkling of the service bell. I sit up alert in my chair wondering what could be wrong. Herr von Konig seldom summons me, but I am on my feet and in the dining room within seconds. As I enter my heart flutters when his ocean blue eyes take me into their gaze.

"Yes, Herr von Konig," I furrow my brows, "Is everything alright? Was your breakfast not warm...the coffee?" He smirks, but with soft eyes.

"No Victoire, everything is–*was* perfect, as usual," he says to me in a calming tone, trying to reduce the anxiety he can see written on my face. It works. My brow relaxes as I look at him trying to slow my breathing to a normal rate.

"Tonight, I have yet another event to attend in the city," I swallow trying not to show my disappointment.

"I understand Monsieur," I nod once.

"I have two surgeries today and will probably not make it back at a decent time to prepare, I would like it if you would assist me and lay out my formal dress for me, pressed, and metals shined. I know it is much to ask of you among the other duties you carry out, but I--"

"Non, Monsieur," I stop him, "It is my pleasure to serve you." I don't know why I say those words. They seemed to fly from my lips on wings, and I couldn't catch them to bring them back and scold them for being so eager to leave me...but I see a light flicker behind his eyes, almost a blaze.

"Shall I teach you pleasure?" he asks.

My breath sticks in my throat and my mind draws a blank. I quickly pull myself together feeling my nipples harden at his words. Suddenly I'm grateful for the new apron I'm wearing that swallows my upper body.

"I'm sorry Herr von Konig," I blink my eyes and shake my head skittishly "can you repeat what you said?" He smirks again, his eyes still on me, penetrating.

"Shall I teach you *pleasure*, Victoire? Would you like to learn to say the word in German?" His plush pink lips turn upward in a smile, hiding his teeth from me.

I breathe out, "Oh! Yes!" remembering our conversation about languages many nights before, "Of course, German...do you have time?"

"Certainly," he assures me with another smile, his gleaming white teeth making my knees tremble under my skirt; it's like watching the sunrise. "It's only one word," he chuckles.

"Yes, please." I too smile bright and slow, biting my lip. He stands from his chair and glides to me, *two steps*, standing himself only inches away from my body, his shoulders blocking out the rays of the cold sun. An electric pulse clicks on in my chest, the buzz is loud and fervid. I fight to stand still, to not shiver when he places his fingers under my chin, gently lifting my face towards his. I almost close my eyes when his warm breath hits the tip of my nose and I quietly inhale the smell of coffee, mint and marmalade.

"Listen, and watch my lips closely," he says softly, placing the pad of his thumb on my chin, *"Ver-gnü-gen."* [*Pleasure.*] I watch his lips and tongue as they make delicious shapes, while fairy dust floats on the deep, soft waves of his voice into my ears. I suck my bottom lip into my mouth just as he pinches and tugs at my chin lightly, "Shall we say it together?" I nod slowly, and we begin in unison. *"Ver-gnü-gen."* The edges of his lips pull upward ever so slightly.

"Again," he quietly commands, the tip of his thumb now drawing tiny circles underneath my chin.

"Oui," I nod.

Again, our voices whisper, "*Ver-gnü-gen*." I lift my eyes from his lips, journeying slowly upwards to stare into the oceans I wish to swim.

"Now that you know how, you must say it to me again, in German, ja?" I nod and obey his request.

"It is my *Vergnügen* to serve you." His eyes darken, setting off rapid pulsations between my legs. He moves his lips to my ear and I feel the first droplets of dew wetting my silk taps. I close my eyes for a brief moment as he whispers to me.

"You are an excellent study Victoire, and it is my *Vergnügen* to teach you. I will be home by eight." He takes a step back from me and picks up his cap from the table, then his lunch, tucking it in his inner coat pocket as the cold sun comes back into view. My eyes dart around me, and my body screams to me "*where did the warmth go...bring it back*!" I fail to oblige its command until I feel him standing behind me. Butterflies awaken from their slumber in my belly, and goosebumps race each other throughout my body. Instinctively I lean my head forward, offering him the nape of my neck.

"Thank you, Victoire," he breathes into my flesh, then brushes his hand ever so slightly down the side of my waist. I gasp. The brief contact sends an electrical surge through my core that stirs my body, and before I can turn to give him my welcome, he is down the corridor, passed the kitchen...passed the sitting room...into the vestibule, fetching his coat, and off into the cold sun, shutting the door behind him. For the second time this morning, my heart sinks.

14

PARTIES

7:45pm
In a blue room
With amber light

THE HOME OF HERR VON KONIG

Victoire

My ears perk to the sound of Herr von Konig's car rolling slowly over the round gravel driveway. I look up briefly toward the window across from the bed as images of Herr von Konig stepping from his car, his broad shoulders sagging wearily from the day, drift through my mind. The short vision flusters me, and my hands begin to shake as I try to lay out his clothes on his bed. Per his request, I have prepared his occasion uniform, spending half the morning shining his shoes, then taking my time to shine his medals. I would be remiss to say that I didn't wonder what each pin and medal were for, and how he had come about them, but in the back of my mind, I suspected they were for reasons I'd rather not think about. Was this a monster that I served? A monster that just by the sound of his voice makes my body ache for him?

I hear his heavy footsteps ascending the stairs as I take one more look over the long grey length of his pants, I bend forward and brush away a few imagined particles with my hand. Just as soon as I raise myself to leave, I feel his presence at the door. Butterflies once again awaken in my belly and the air in the room grows thin. A sudden heat moves over my ears, muffling sound, and my neck strains to make up for the suppression of my senses. I turn and see him leaning against the door, watching me closely. So tall, solemn, and beautiful, with slicked-back hair like soie de maïs [*cornsilk*]. His eyes sweep along my body and I'm embarrassed as I believe he can see the evidence of my excitement, the blood pumping through the veins in my neck and the indentations of my hardened nipples through my apron. Herr von Konig tilts his head slightly, looking behind me to his uniform and polished shoes. In three strides he reaches my side, where he closely reviews my work.

He keeps his eyes on the uniform as he speaks to me in his resonant, yet soothing voice, "Exceptional work, Thank you Victoire." *I am drowning in honey*. Herr von Konig places two fingers under the lapel of the jacket and glides them downward forcing the small medals to jump and gleam in the amber light. I smile knowing he is pleased.

"Your overnight satchel is packed Monsieur," he nods sternly acknowledging the brown leather bag at the foot of the bed, "and I have drawn you a bath." Herr von Koning's head lifts with a snap, his eyebrows furrow in surprise.

"Really!?" he questions with muted excitement. I nod my head, parting my lips to smile, but when I see the sparkle in his eyes, I bite my bottom lip against the force of those blue oceans as they wash over me. As if his eyes weren't enough to send me drifting away, his fingers fly to his collar and he begins to remove his tie, unbuttoning his shirt. My breathing becomes labored at the sight of him releasing each button from its cotton cage. I know he is speaking to me, but I can't make out the words as the muffled heat assaults my ears again, impairing my hearing. My eyes are fixed on his Adam's apple, watching how it bobs up and down behind the smooth creamy flesh of his throat. I struggle against the urgent craving to wrap my arms around his neck, posture my lips over the round cartilage, and nurse from it like a baby. The appetite to taste him stings the glands on either side of my tongue, and I swallow the salivation that forms, hoping he doesn't notice my response to his movements. Herr von Koning never takes his eyes from mine as he completes his task, and with the last button undone, he takes a step toward me, waking me from the fantasy unfurling before me with a jump. His heat bears down on me, emanating from his chest like a furnace, pulling tiny glistening beads of sweat from my body. My ears finally open.

"You've done more than I asked of you, Victoire, I am grateful. ...Victoire? Victoire, are you alright?" His face now a mask of concern, he reaches out and encircles my arms with his hands, nimble and sturdy. Even his touch burns hot. It's too much for me to take and I feel faint. I slowly shrug my arms trying to free myself of his grip.

"Yes, Monsieur. I'm sorry, I'm fine, of-of course." He chuckles at me, giving my arms a gentle squeeze before removing his hands, then turning to walk to the bathroom, slipping his feet out of his shoes, and removing his belt, letting it drop to the floor with a quiet 'clang'.

"What did I say about apologizing...it doesn't become

you," he calls. When he enters the bathroom he stops at the sink looking at the comb, clippers and cologne I set out for him. I had taken a moment before laying out his uniform to sniff a few of the elegant bottles on his dresser. I was missing my own vanity that was once filled with lipstick, pictures of my parents, postcards from friends and colorful crystalline bottles of expensive parfum. When I came across the bottle with the gold cursive script that read *Agrume de Foncé*, I unscrewed the top and was instantly transported to the day he saved me, the day he brought me to his home. I remembered how his aroma of bergamot, sweet orange and clove mixed pleasantly with the balmy scent of the white roses at the fountain, heady and succulent. I step backward, foot behind foot retreating quietly from his room and closing the door behind me. I turn quickly and make my way to the kitchen to finish preparing my supper.

Emil

AS I EYE the cologne that Victoire has set out for me, I hear the door click on the other side of the room. I look up and see that Victoire has made her exit. For one brief moment life with my specter was real. Having her in my room touching my things was exhilarating, though I reigned in my delight as much as I could muster. When I walked in, seeing her bent over my bed gently dragging her hand down my uniform, I had to adjust my cock. The sight of her in such a position set off a flame in my chest and groin. I turned my attention to my uniform. She had done a wonderful job making everything look so pristine, I don't think I've ever gotten my medals and shoes to shine as she has.

It must have taken a while to do, knowing that Victoire

has never done domestic work before. The idea floats around in my head that she must really enjoy pleasing me or maybe she takes pride in her work, I'm hoping it's not just the latter because I want her, and if her efforts are a reflection of the small German lesson we had this morning then I know she must feel something for me. *What a silly line of thinking, from shoes to desire.* I shake my head at my thought process then pick up the bottle of cologne, it's the same scent I wore the day Rolf and I helped her escape the foot soldiers. *Had she noticed or was this a random choice?* I close the door to the bathroom, then pull off my pants and underwear. I sink a foot into the bath that Victoire has prepared for me and the water temperature is perfect.

I sit, closing my eyes and letting the steam roll over me. I can hear some version of ``La Tristesse de Saint Louis'' coming from Victoire's little radio in the kitchen, soft and distant. It makes me wonder if she misses music and singing, more than that, her life before Vichy Régime. She was free once, though I don't claim to hold her prisoner. She had a home, a family, even a little place in the countryside a few miles from here. The day Rolf and I picked her up, we went to her little cottage and packed some bags for her. I pulled many of her silk underpinnings, which she later was surprised to find tucked under a few dresses and sheets. I remember the feel of her nightgowns between my fingers. There was this one pair of knickers, so light and dainty with tiny bows and lace at the bottom, when Rolf left the room to find some blankets and other comforts, I brought them to my nose and inhaled deeply, and like a sick fuck, I licked the inner seam hoping to taste her. I shoved them in my breast pocket before we left.

The thought of Victoire on my tongue brings me to a familiar place with my hand wrapped around my cock, slowly squeezing and stroking its length. My mind drifts to the night I saw her in the pink lounge, her dress barely covering her glowing pecan skin. I stroke faster, the tingle in my spine growing hot. Finally, my mind pulls this morning's German lesson out of reserve when I watched her lips as she told me it was her pleasure to serve me. The vision throws me over the edge and I grit my teeth as I cum hard. I watch through hooded lids as my thick white seed spurts up and runs down over my hand and into the water.

"Ah, fuck. Victoire," I whisper. I wait a few minutes to catch my breath, then with a sigh, I reach down to unplug the drain. Once the water is low I turn on the faucet, soap up a cloth and wash my body. Thirty minutes later, overnight satchel in hand, I make my way downstairs and to the kitchen where Victoire is sitting quietly reading one of the magazines she requested I buy for her.

"I am leaving now." Victoire stands, giving me a demure smile and a nod, following me to the vestibule. I reach for my coat, but before I can retrieve it from the rack Victoire has the collar in her hands.

"Allow me Monsieur." I turn my back to her as she brings the coat down to meet my hands, then slides the wool sleeves over my arms and shoulders. She steps around to my front and tugs the lapels, checking to make sure they are straight. Placing one hand inside my coat, she buttons the one inner button, smoothing the material downward with a firm but gentle swoosh. She steps closer, lowering her head, focusing intently and buttons the two outer buttons. I can feel the slight tremble in her hands against my torso. I place my hand on hers, but she lets them fall away and takes a step back, her eyes still on the ground.

"Tha-," before I can get out my words she interrupts.

"Non, Monsieur. No need to thank me. Enjoy your evening."

She reaches to the top shelves above the coat rack and pulls down my shearling gloves, handing them to me with another demure smile. I nod, not knowing what to say. Moments later I am in the car heading toward the city, wishing I were home listening for my ghost, Victoire.

Victoire

I RUB my hands together trying to keep myself warm. My bath was nice and hot and the tin of olive oil I poured in has left my skin hydrated and smooth, I saved a little in a cup to rub into my skin and fingernails after I dried off. I rummage through my dresser and find a white silk gown I bought in Paris. I had it custom made by a couturier I met years ago. Madame Reynard keeps my measurements on file and when I want something pretty, she whips it up. This was meant to be for a special night with someone, but that someone didn't quite work out, so I got rid of him...not the negligee. Bias cut silk wraps my body like a glove; she added little crystal beads on the thin, string-like, straps that drape over my shoulders. The neckline dips into a plunging wide 'V', meant to slip a little and show just a hint of, well...you know. There is a low cowl in the back and a long train of French handmade lace that trails when I walk. Yes, this cost me a pretty penny. I was surprised to find it at the bottom of the luggage that Herr von Konig and Herr Bliss brought back for me from my cottage.

I was a little embarrassed to see almost the whole of my lingerie collection folded delicately under my clothes and some blankets. I am missing a pair of silk taps I had made with little bows and lace at the bottom, but I'm sure they weren't able or interested in bringing everything I owned.

I'm glad to have something that reminds me that once, not but a few months ago, I was Victoire Duplanchier, international singer, debuting in nightclubs, restaurants and lounges all over the world. Now, I am just Victoire, a maid, with only a ghost and a little boy who lives in the woods to keep her company. But tonight, I decide to treat myself as the former. My hair is pressed, so I comb it and pin it up. I wrap a blanket around my shivering body to make my way to the den. Something is missing though, *parfum*. How I miss wearing parfum. My collection was in my apartment in Paris, I didn't go back and retrieve them, I thought I'd have time to make another trip. I was wrong.

I make my way upstairs and slip into Herr von Konig's room, turning on the amber lights, and I spot his bottle of *Agrume de Foncé, the scent that would have me follow him through the gates of hades*; I dab a bit on my wrist and neck. I smell like him. Warm, masculine and luscious. I feel the familiar throbbing between my legs as I walk out of his blue room, running my hand along the edge of his bed. My viscous essence spreads from back to front, with each step. I stop at the door and stretch my body as it begs me for a release. *Later*. I want to fully enjoy my evening.

I enter the den. I love this room; it reflects the aesthetic of Herr von Konig so well. The fireplace is large, and the dark brown leather furniture is inviting. A tan and cream hide rug lays in front of the hearth. I take a few moments to make a fire. I made sure everything was in place this morning, cleaning out the flue and adding a few logs from the woodpile out back. I watch as it begins to roar. *If only I could sleep here every night*. I clap my hands, spin around in a circle and look around the den. In five months, Herr von Konig has managed to fill a good majority of the walls with books, art and records. I pull down one of his photo albums and lay it on the rug, it will be my reading for the night. I head back to the shelves and flip through the records. I'm shocked when I see he has the first album I ever recorded, the *only* album I ever recorded. Everything was in place for a 2nd record, but then the war came to Paris. I lift the top on the record player, fix myself a brandy, then pull the black vinyl disk from its jacket and place it under the needle. In mere seconds, like a bell, my voice rings through the speaker...and I weep, falling to the hide rug.

Emil

"OBERSTARZT VON KONIG, how nice of you to join us!" a short squishy faced woman says to me as she extends her hand in my direction. I smile leaning my head to Rolf who picks up on my cue.

"Emil, may I introduce you to Frau Schröder, she is not only the most beautiful woman in all of Paris but also the wife of our gracious host Oberleutnant Fritz Schröder." Frau Schröder smiles and giggles at Rolf's introduction, he always did know how to lay it on thick. I capture her extended hand and kiss the air around it, she giggles even more.

"Oh, Lt. Bliss..." Rolf interrupts her gushing, holding up his palm.

"Rolf. Please, a beauty like you should not have to use such titles."

"Ah,haa,ha,haaa," she laughs loudly, drawing attention to our presence from two very familiar faces, I squint my eyes trying to remember where I know them from, then it hits me.

They were the two officers that passed by Rolf and me the day we found Victoire.

"Shhhit," I mumble under my breath.

"E-excuse me?" Frau Schröder asks with surprised questioning, "Did you say something, my dear?"

The sound of her voice drowns out as the two men make their way over to me and Rolf.

Rolf smiles and takes her hand, "Shoes, madam. I believe our friend here was admiring your shoes," Rolf smiles.

"Oh! Why thank you, I had them handmade here in Paris, wouldn't you know the first day we moved in..." her voice trails off into the air as the faces grow closer. "Ah!," she pauses as the officers come into her view, "Lt. Jäger and Lt. Keller, may I introduce you to –" she is cut off by the one she introduces as Lt. Jäger.

"Yes, our resident surgeon, Oberstarzt von Konig and his friend Lt. Bliss! Do forgive me Maria, but we had the pleasure of meeting them some months ago on the street. You were in a spot of trouble, ja!?," he smirks, sarcasm thick. I hate him already.

"No trouble, just a misunderstanding," I retort, staring him dead in the eye, feeling Rolf move to my side.

"Yeees, yeees," he smiles, though the brightness doesn't reach his eyes. He rolls them up in the air as if trying to find a word, then snaps his fingers as if having an epiphany, "the negerfrau."

I see Frau Schröder's brow line furrow and her hand flies to her lips, no doubt in shock to learn that her guest has had any association with a black woman. My fist balls at my side as I feel fire running up my neck. I take half a step forward but Rolf slaps his hand on my shoulder with a loud laugh, drawing attention from everyone, ultimately exploiting our situation in order to avoid a confrontation.

"No need for shock Frau Schröder," Rolf explains, "it was indeed a misunderstanding. As you know Oberstarzt von Konig acquired a rather sizable estate and needed a maid, the young lady refused and just needed a bit of convincing, that is all." Frau Schröder smiles at Rolf's explanation. *Simpleton.*

She giggles, "Well I'm sure you could have found a nice young French or German girl to assist you!?"

"Heaven's no," Rolf feigns shock, "and have the world's most beautiful Mädchen scrubbing floors and hauling rubbish, I think not." Rolf extends his elbow for her, guiding her away from the conversation and further into the party.

"Emil, will you join us?" Frau Schröder calls over her shoulder, "I want to introduce you to my husband." I nod my head to the two men and walk away. They don't outrank me, so I don't have to salute, *thank God.*

The party wares on for hours with a constant flow of stuffed shirts, cigars, talk of the next invasion and the Führer's designs for Paris. I'm so fucking done. I look at my watch, and it's not as late as I thought. I'm tired and though Victoire packed my overnight satchel, the last thing I want to do is sleep in one of the surgical beds in my office. I could stay with Rolf but he's already three sheets to the wind, and I don't care to take up residence with him while he's drunk. It's a 30-minute drive back home, through the fucking woods, but I haven't been drinking and the thought of Victoire's warm honey cake sways my decision. I'm going home tonight.

Rolf is in the corner with a scowl on his face. I need to get him out of here before he says something he'll regret, or not. He's good at wearing the mask when he's sober, but when he's drunk it's Russian Roulette. I make my apologies to the hostess and walk across the room to Rolf.

"von Konig!"

Fuck. Jäger.

"I hope I didn't cause a fuss earlier this evening," he laughs. I suck my teeth, an involuntary reaction and immediately regret it, setting my jaw. "I should like to come visit." His green eyes sparkle with diabolical mirth. This man has done many bad things and feels nothing; he has eyes like my father. I see Rolf stand and begin walking towards us. "Our fathers know each other, I've recently learned. It would be nice to send an endearing report home letting them know that we've at least dined together, don't you think?" My eyes widen and the red mist begins to descend. Rolf steps in, answering for me.

"Yes, why don't we meet at Miette's?" Jäger turns his hard eyes to Rolf.

"I said nothing about you Neureich." This time it is Rolf who needs a slap on the shoulder, his body is tense and his hollowed cheeks tell me he is about to unload a pile of verbal offal. I step in front of him.

"Yes, Jäger let's meet at Miette's. I could use a good night out and some entertainment."

Jäger turns his attention back to me, again giving me a shallow smile.

"Ah, you see, tsk, tsk, I eat out almost every night," he sighs heavily, "I should like to have a nice home-cooked meal, I'm sure our fathers would love to know that we are being properly, shall we say, taken care of." I know what he's hinting at, Rolf moves behind me gritting his teeth.

"No," he whispers.

Jäger only chuckles. "Tomorrow night, shall we say 8 o'clock? Don't worry, I'll get your address. Oh, and you're little lap dog can come too, I see you two are attached at the hip," his eyes dart back and forth between me and Rolf, daring us to say anything just as Frau Schröder approaches our little party of three. "Well now, Maria! It was so nice seeing you, you lovely thing," Jäger feigns as he places her hand under his arm, "We must do this again! Now, my mother would absolutely love the recipe for the chicken you served tonight..."

I turn to Rolf, and I see him walking out the door. I try to catch up, but his driver is already closing his car door. They take off down the street. Within minutes, I'm heading home.

A FIRE

In a darkened den
In a manor on the countryside
A small fire burns

THE HOME OF HERR VON KONIG

Emil

Halfway through my drive home, I'm cursing myself. The woods are dark and winding, and I hate to drive at night. The only alternative is to turn back, and what's the point in that. Fifteen minutes and a few twists and turns later, I pull into the driveway. As I approach the round, I see a small amber glow through the window of my den. The windows in the rest of the house are dark; I'm curious to see what is happening while I'm supposed to be away. I leave my satchel on the seat and close the car door quietly, bumping it with my hip to secure the latch without a loud thud. I enter the vestibule as quietly as I can, removing my shoes, they make the most dreadful thwacking noise against the wood floors. I make my way through the corridor, then turn to my den to see the most fascinating sight. *Victoire.* She lies, sleeping peacefully, on her back on top of my hide rug, in a delicate white silk gown that barely covers her generous breasts. Her chest rises and falls gently with each breath. My eyes drink her in as if they have been devoid of hydration for centuries. The low burning light of the fire travels over her shining skin, creating a glow that can only be described as empyrean, her parted lips and closed almond-sculpted eyes giving her face a celestial beauty.

I remove my gloves and coat, placing them quietly on the leather kanapee across from her, never taking my eyes off the beauty before me. Should I wake her, and inquire as to why she's sleeping in the den? Should I turn and leave, head back to the city, and return tomorrow as we discussed, never mentioning what I've seen? The fire burns lower and I notice her shiver. I walk over to the hearth and toss in another log, turning it with the poker until the flames rise high and the room fills with a bright burning light. I turn my attention back to Victoire. I sit on the hearth and place my head in my hands, ruminating deeply about tomorrow. That prick Jäger will be coming not for dinner, but for trouble. There's no way to avoid it. I don't want him anywhere near Victoire. I saw the way he eyed her that day, it was a mix of disgust and curious interest. *It'll be fine. What's the worst that could happen?* Rolf and I will both be here. All she need do is set out dinner then I will excuse her for the evening; I won't give him time to develop any further interest. Victoire stirs and I quiet my thoughts, staring at her hoping she doesn't wake. I don't want to scare her, and mostly I feel like I've invaded her privacy. I decide to retire for the evening, walking past

Victoire in my stocking feet. Just as I reach the door, I hear it.

"Emil."

She whispers my name and my blood pounds in my ears. I turn back to answer her, but her eyes are still closed. I shake my head not believing that what I heard was real. I start to leave again, but this time I am positive about what I hear. She is talking in her sleep, the tiniest softest coo, "Emil...yes." I run my fingers through my hair nervously and make my way back to my Angel. I whisper her name, lying down on my stomach an arm's length from her. What I witness next blows my mind. My Angel arches her back, and my eyes widen with wonder, her head thrashing side to side gently and she bites her bottom lip. Her arms glide up on either side of her head, her palms facing upward, she arches her back again with another tiny coo, "Ah." My heart is pounding in my chest, and my jaw ticks, I want to answer her, she's calling for me.

The thin material of her nightdress does nothing to hide her arousal, the tips of her breasts begin to firm underneath her diaphanous gown and her heavy breathing forces the deep wide 'V' to push outward giving me a full view of one glorious toasted golden bud. It takes all the strength I can muster not to wrap my arm around her waist, pull her to me and suckle the morsel in between my lips. I lick the salivation from the corner of my mouth. "Hhah, Emil, yes." Another arch, and this time her knees pull up, her legs resting on the balls of her feet as they spread wide. I can smell her. I tamp down a growl, and just as my resolve begins to weaken, she turns over to her stomach away from me, giving me a view of her beautiful back. The long hollow line of her spine sways down and outward to her round ass, plentiful and shaped like a juicy pear, two dimples greet me as I realize her vivid chimera isn't over. Her fingers bite into the hide rug and her right leg pulls upward, her hips begin to move slowly forward and back.

"Please," she begs, her voice so low I almost miss it. Her slow rocking soon picks up speed.

Fuck, fuck, fuck.

I watch with bated breath, my cock is stiff, straining against the metal buttons of my pants. A dull cramp creeps into my fingers. My hands literally ache to touch her, to answer her pleadings for me to take her. All I have to do is reach out and wake her, then fuck her slow until she cums as many times as her body can stand, right here in front of the fire. Her scent grows stronger and I know her efforts are bringing her close. She's panting, whispering "yes", cooing my name and then it happens.

"Aah, aah, ahh," her body trembles and her perfect pear-shaped ass is making the most erotic jiggles and ticks as her release runs through her. I reach down to my member and squeeze, forcing myself to calm the fuck down. I sit up and grab my hair in my hands, sniffing the air quietly as I can, savoring the musky, powdery scent of her pussy and...and my cologne, how did I not notice it before. *My God this woman is wearing my cologne and calling my name in a wet dream.* She stretches her body, like a lazy kitten sunning itself in a window, then to add to my frustration, she pops a finger in her mouth, sucking sweetly, seductively and then nothing but tiny snores follow. I'm unable to move from my spot next to her on the floor for long moments, when I finally will myself away, the sun is beginning to rise. I pour myself two fingers of scotch, shoot it back, stoke the fire once more to keep her warm, then pass out on the couch. It's been a very, very long night.

Victoire

MY BODY IS STIFF. With my eyes still closed, I arch my back upward and hear it crack, "Ah, Chérie...you are getting old, non," I giggle to myself. I yawn and rub my eyes, looking at the mess I've made on the floor. Two blankets lie twisted at my feet, an empty glass of brandy, that I filled twice last night, and one of Herr von Konig's family photo albums. I shake my head, looking one last time at a photograph of Herr von Konig standing next to a man that could be his twin, only 20 years older. He's handsome, but the scowl on his face makes my heart hurt for Herr von Konig. It's a graduation picture, and though everyone else in the background is smiling with their families he and his father stare blankly into the camera. I shrug my shoulders, shut the book with a loud *whhop*, then commence to folding the blankets at my feet. I rise to my knees, look down and see my gown has slipped off, exposing my breast.

"Hmm," I hum quietly to myself, remembering last night. After my fit of tears and my second glass of brandy, I flipped through Herr von Konig's photograph book, found a photo of him smiling into the camera and let his eyes work me into a frenzy. I was wet the moment I dabbed on his cologne last night, I just prolonged my pleasure. *Maybe once more before I begin my day?* I think to myself. I bring my finger to my mouth, wetting it then slowly trace over my bare peak, "mmm," I moan, letting the feeling wash over me, wetness returns between my legs and a sultry throbbing begins at my clit, as it yearns to be touched. I sit, preparing myself to lay back when I look over to the fireplace. It's still burning fairly bright, which is odd. I know it's dangerous to fall asleep when a fire is still going, but I passed out after I came, practically screaming Herr von Konig's name. I look closer and the poker is laying on the hearth, not back in the holder where I know I left it. *Oh, no!*

My blood freezes and the muffling heat descends around my ears creating the feeling of pins and needles from my neck to scalp. I turn slowly to my left and there laid out on the canapé is Herr von Konig. I almost leap out of my skin. I scramble to pull up my gown and cover my body with the blankets, my own, not the one I pulled off his leather canapé and later in the night, it smelled of him. He lays on his back with his eyes closed and an arm draped over his face blocking the sun that shines through the window, his other arm meets the floor next to a glass he must have drunk during the night. *Oh, no, how long has he been here?* I tiptoe, quickly replacing the photo album and the record back in their place. I pick up my glass and toss the blanket on the club chair. Before I make it off the rug, his voice cuts through me.

"Victoire." He remains in his place, his arm still over his eyes. The blonde hairs on his sinewy forearm sparkle like little diamonds in the light.

"Oui, Monsieur," I answer with a whisper as if the softness of my voice would make a difference in my fate. At my reply he removes his arm, lifting up his torso from the canapé and placing his feet on the floor. He draws his hands down his face clasping them together. Leaning forward with his forearms on his knees he looks at me hard, his chiseled jaw firm beneath his 5 o'clock shadow. *Why does he sweep over my body with those eyes?*

"Why were you sleeping in here?"

"Monsieur, I--. Please forgive me for abusing your home and overstepping my position, my room is almost freezing at night." He furrows his brows at my answer and nods once slowly.

"Did you enjoy your evening by the fire?" I wince at the

question, not knowing how to answer. I should not have complained, I have a roof over my head. Herr von Konig should be able to trust that when he leaves his home his maid isn't taking advantage of it, and yet, the one time I do, he returns home early without ceremony. I am both embarrassed and afraid. Though I am not really a maid, Herr von Konig saved my life and my position here guarantees my safety, if I lose it I don't know where I'll go. Of course there is my cottage, but I cannot be sure that it's safe, especially just me alone. I make a quick decision for my answer.

"I am sorry, Monsieur."

He continues to stare like he can see through me, see my heart pounding in my chest, see my mind racing through every scenario I can think of for what I will do when, and if he relieves me of my position. All I can do is wait. He leans back, throwing his arm over the back of the chair, and placing his ankle over his knee. He smirks at me, then licks his lips.

"Apologizing again, Victoire? It really is beneath you," my eyes widen at his response, "Shall I ask my question again?" He stands up from the couch and strides over to me confident and tiger-like. His massive frame blots out the sun. He situates himself only an inch away, his body heat ebbing my energy. I look up for a full view of the most mesmeric face. I strain against the need to run the back of my fingers over his lips, pink and plump shaded by a cornsilk blonde mustache just tickling his upper lip. If only I could just caress the space between his brows and smooth out the anger lines or hold my hand over his cheek and graze back and forth between rubbing the lobe of his ear and gently brushing his jaw.

I breathe deeply, feeling myself swaying toward him. He reaches out his hand and gently tugs away my blanket; I let it fall without hesitation or argument. He continues to look me in my eyes as I feel one finger tap and land on my collarbone. "Victoire," his finger is moving ever so slowly across my clavicle. He has not released his gaze, "Did you enjoy your evening?" I'm so wet, and I know he can see my arousal through the gossamer material of my gown. I want this man. I want him over me, behind me, inside me, "I'm waiting for your answer, Angel."

Angel.

I feel the tiny beaded strap of my gown fall away. My eyes close and I brush my cheek against my shoulder. "Oui, Monsieur...yes," I whisper. A low growl escapes from his throat.

"Move your things, tonight, to one of the guest bedrooms upstairs. Take your pick." I shake my head in protest, but he growls again, "It is done." His hand captures my waist bringing me into him where I feel his need against my waist. His finger flicks my nipple softly as he lowers...

BANG! BANG! BANG! BANG! BANG!

Heavy pounding on the oak front door snaps me out of my trance. I drop to the floor quickly to pick up my blanket and I run from the den, leaving Herr von Konig behind.

Emil

VICTOIRE SLIPS THROUGH MY FINGERS. Her scent hovers in the spot where she just stood. I close my eyes and lean in to inhale. The door bangs again. I grunt my disappointment while making my way to the door, *whomever this is better have a fucking good reason.* I swing the door open hard, creating a suction that almost pulls Rolf forward into the vestibule.

"Tell me you're not doing this tonight," Rolf questions,

walking straight passed me into the house, "tell me, you thought it over last night and you've decided to decline Jäger's self-appointed invitation for dinner?" I grimace at his words and slam the door shut. I huff passed my friend, smoothing my tousled hair back with one pass. I shake my head, not knowing what else to do.

"Shhhitt, Emil," Rolf whispers disapprovingly, "you know exactly what that little shit is up to, and you're just going to allow it? Let Victoire go for the night. She can come and stay with me, I'll leave her there, and return for dinner. I can spirit her in and out of the apartment easily." I can barely think, not but three seconds ago I was touching Victoire's soft pecan skin, and now Rolf is at my throat like it's the Spanish-fucking-inquisition. "Have you even told her yet?"

"Herr Bliss!"

Victoire enters the foyer, fully dressed with a smile. Rolf returns her smile with one just as bright. Once she reaches him, he takes her hand and kisses it softly, looking at me out of the corner of his eye with a crooked grin. He knows how jealous I am of *them* and enjoys toying with me. Victoire giggles, as he taps his fingers on her forehead.

"My lovely Victoire, how would you like to come and spend an evening in the city? We won't be able to go anywhere, as you know," his voice is sorrowful, "but I'll order for you from Miette's, and set up a film. I have a projector," he gloats shamelessly, "and Hitchcock's *Jamaica Inn*. I'll make a night of it for you. Pack whatever you like for the evening and come with me." I don't interrupt my friend's request, this is the best for her, and she would love an evening of fancy food and a picture show. Victoire smiles wide and her eyes dance, then I can see she's beginning to piece the offer together.

"Will it be, just me," she asks skeptically.

Rolf nods 'yes.'

"Alone?" Rolf and I look at each other, his lips purse together as he answers her.

"Yes, unfortunately alone."

Victoire scrunches her face, "Why?"

I decide to give up the charade. "I have a guest coming for dinner, it's business and we thought it would be best if maybe you weren't here for the evening?" Her face is stoic as she looks us both over.

"I will stay and start preparing supper." She turns on her heels toward the kitchen.

Rolf and I shout in unison, "Victoire!" and we both reach out for her, but she spins around quickly, waving her hand in the air signaling 'enough.'

"You'll forgive me if I forget my place, but I'd rather not spend an evening in the city alone. I spend enough time alone, always in this big house alone, daytime alone, night alone. Tonight, business or no, there will be company, discussion, footsteps, possible laughter, it would be nice to hear sound again, and not that of my own breathing! Now, I will go to prepare." She leaves us, both gobsmacked in the middle of the foyer, neither of us having the heart to argue with her. We resolve to make the evening as pleasant as possible, if only for Victoire. We keep on our toes knowing that Jäger has a design he is hell-bent on fashioning out.

We both leave for the city. I have a few Saturday patients and Rolf an impromptu meeting on North African relations at the Intelligence office. I lose myself in my work and put my anxieties about tonight aside, for the moment.

LÈVRES ROUGES

In a clawfoot tub
Of a warm bathroom
In a new room

Victoire

I make the maximum effort to close this morning's incident between Herr von Konig and me in a box, in the back of my mind. I grip the side of the tub until I feel the sharp edges begin to press deep into my fingers. I grit my teeth and squint my eyes shut hard.

"Eeerrrrrr!"

I take a deep breath and calm myself. *It was nothing, and that's the end of it.*

My efforts triumph when I deeply inhale the smell of the honey cake I pulled from the oven around 6 o'clock, Herr von Konig's favorite. I rinse the egg yolks from my hair, and smile to myself as I step from the bath, wrapping a towel around my body. Per his insistence, I found a moment or two to move a few of my things into one of the upstairs rooms. My bed is made and the hearth is warm. It's beautiful. Aside from that, I have spent the entire day cooking for our dinner guest, who should be arriving within the hour along with Herr von Konig and Herr Bliss. I must admit that I wish to please Herr Bliss almost as much as Herr von Konig. Each time I encounter him he has been more than kind and sweet to me, always asking if I'm keeping well, and when I answer *yes* his face lights up like a schoolboy as if my answer has made his day. He is like Herr von Konig in some ways, very tall, handsome as the day is long and somber, but with light brown hair, and a cleft chin. In his smile, there is a hint of sadness, like he's searching for something precious that's been lost. I pray one day he finds this precious thing. I fear it will kill him if he does not. His invitation for me to stay in the city was lovely, but alone? For months I haven't had the heart to tell him how lonely I am. The joy in his face from my simple reply compels me to keep my melancholia to myself, but today was the final pin.

I sigh as I look at myself in the mirror. I'm happy for there to be company, for there to be laughter and conversation floating to the kitchen. However, Herr von Konig doesn't seem to share my sentiment. He's made his business acquaintance seem more like an intruder than a welcomed guest. His reservations give me pause. I understand them, I am not without knowledge of the possible nature of his guest, yet the oppressive nature of my loneliness clouds my better judgement, and I can't seem to shake my delight. I went to work making a roast with root vegetables after my gentlemen left the house this morning. I even baked a loaf of bread, half of which I set out for my little friend with a full jar of jam, which were both gone by the early afternoon. *One day I will catch my Little Rabbit,* I giggle to myself, and I will hug him, and kiss his little smiling cheeks. Maybe even bring him to live with us. *Us?* I squint hard again and slam the lid tighter on the box in the back of my mind. I look at my little travel clock, *7:30.* I hurry and braid my dark woolen hair into a crown around my head and for the occasion, I add a dash of rouge lipstick, pressing my defined lips together and swiping them over each other to disperse the color. I flick off the bathroom light and turn to my room, just before I cross the threshold, I grab the lipstick again and add a dab of color to each cheek blending as I make my way to my new closet.

Fifteen minutes later I am back in the dining room. I set the table for a formal dinner, thanking my most recent housekeeping magazine for their diagram. I'd never set a table before for anything more than a cup of coffee or tea in the mornings, my family always had Lisette our maid do that. When I traveled, I had a girl who traveled with me to prepare my clothes and meals and travel arrangements, but I let her go the moment we returned from Marrakech, she was worried about her family too and needed to go be with them in Portugal. I finish setting the last glass when I hear the door opening in the vestibule. I wipe my hands down the front of my apron and make my way to greet. I hear the low voices of Herr von Konig and Herr Bliss. When I step through the door to take their coats, Herr von Konig freezes, staring at me wide-eyed as if he'd seen a ghost. Immediately I am nervous and begin to fidget with the collar of my apron.

"Good Evening Herr von Konig," I try and offer a natural smile, but I fail. I change my focus to Herr Bliss, giving him a small curtsey, my smile genuine. "Monsieur," Herr Bliss smiles back. "May I take your coat?" Herr Bliss's eyes soften as he shakes his head.

"No, Victoire, thank you, I've got it." He continues to

stare at me too, pulling off his coat and hanging it on the rack. Herr von Konig's eyes are burning into me so hotly I hesitate before I turn to him again. When I do, I jump back surprised as he is mere inches away, bent over me, glaring. I can only look at his chest, as my nervousness returns. *Is it my hair? Is my makeup too much?* I bring a trembling hand to my mouth and purse my lips. Herr von Konig growls, just when Herr Bliss steps in front of him gently taking my hand in both of his; *he's so calming and gentle.*

"You look beautiful tonight Victoire, lovely. And might I say woman, this house smells delicious," he turns me slowly heading out of the vestibule, walking me down the corridor toward the dining room leaving Herr von Konig behind. I feel his eyes now burning a hole in my back. Herr Bliss continues his compliments. "Are you quite certain you're not that witch from the fairy story Hansel & Gretel, with your house made of lovely cakes and candies...I would eat this house. I would *if* I didn't know there were termites in the cellar!" We both laugh brightly. Herr Bliss opens the door to the kitchen for me and ushers me in. "Pay no attention to our grumpy friend Victoire," he says while sitting down in a chair at the small round kitchen table, "no doubt it has been a long day for him, and the impending arrival of our guest is wearing on him." I turn from the sink to face Herr Bliss.

"Is his guest that awful as to make him act the way he does? I'll admit Herr von Konig is always a bit brooding and quiet but," I stop myself. If one thing I do know about servants, gossip is never a good idea. I calm myself and give Herr Bliss a closed lip smile, just the edges of my mouth turned upward. "I understand Herr Bliss, I will do all I can to make this evening run smoothly for you both and your guest." His face darkens. He gets up from the table and walks to me, taking both my hands again, and encasing them in his.

"Do me a small favor, Victoire. Serve the meal gracefully as you always do, but quickly. Only come when called, no need to check on us. Once you have finished your duties, stay here in the kitchen or go straight to your room. Can you do this for me?" He looks deeply into my eyes, still holding my hands.

I nod, "Oui, Monsieur." He sighs deeply and kisses them.

"Bon! I shall go check on our cranky friend." He grins and taps his fingers across my forehead. I scrunch my nose and giggle. When he leaves, I turn back to the sink and finish washing out a few of the dishes I used to prepare their meal.

Emil

RED LIPS...PERFUME!? Even without any of it, Victoire is a goddess, with it, she is a goddess attracting the attention of every demon in hell. Her lips are a flag waving in the face of a bull. I want to march into the kitchen and tell her to take it all off, but what would that make me look like. *A small man.* Victoire is her own woman, and I have no wish to order her around...but I don't want to give Jäger any more reason to be interested in her. I stand and stare into the fire Victoire started, whisky glass at my side. I know she's the reason he's coming here tonight, to pry, to sneak. At *that* thought, I change my mind, then turn to go to the kitchen and demand she remove her makeup and wash her neck. I bump into Rolf's chest as he rounds the corner into the den. He doesn't move, instead, he leans inside the door jamb nonchalantly crossing his legs, shooting out his arm cutting me right at my neck.

"...Aaand you are going where?" he asks with a hint of

sarcasm. He knows exactly where I'm going, otherwise, he wouldn't be blocking the door.

"Move." The simple word comes out of my mouth dripping with grit and anger. He moves, but only from one side of the door to the other, playing a game. "I'm not fucking playing with you Rolf," I growl low, but he shakes his head.

"My friend, I have already spoken with her," he says, lowering his voice. My brows shoot up with questioning, "just let her feel like herself tonight. No one ever comes out here to visit, and I believe she is happy to have some company other than the two interminably sour assholes that inhabit this baby mansion...well, *I* don't live here, so she only has the company of *one* interminably sour asshole," he chuckles, pushing two fingers into my chest and walking me backward into the den. Rolf passes by me then flops into the brown leather club chair, sinking down and throwing his leg over the arm. He looks around, irritated, searching for something, then he sees it, a crystal bottle of brandy. He hops up, picks it off the bar cart, then flops back in the chair again.

"You're a lush," I admonish jokingly. He laughs, wiping a few drops of liquor from his chin.

"Fffuck, I know," he says with a chuckle, then all of a sudden the mirth is gone and he stares at the same spot in the fire I had chosen not moments ago, with a bleakness he completes his response, "but it helps." My heart aches for my friend, I don't know why, but it does. To help lighten his burden, I place it back on me.

"What did you say to her?"

He smiles at me, taking another swing.

"Doesn't matter. She looks beautiful as ever and feels beautiful, I can tell. Drop it, Emil. She made her decision to stay. We're both here, she's safe," he flicks his hand at me returning to his drink.

We look at each other when we both hear a vehicle pull up to the house, our silent gaze a promise to each other to remain calm.

The chime rings through the house once, and then the door bangs three times. Before I can leave the den I see Victoire on her way to the vestibule. My eyes widen and I stride quickly to catch her before she reaches the door.

"Victoire," I call to her sternly, "I will answer the door, please go back to the kitchen." The sparkle in her eyes fades, and they shift downward.

"Yes, Herr von Konig," she says, just above a whisper. It kills me to see her disappointed, but I don't want him in such close proximity to her if I can help it. He is a dog looking for a bone. "Dinner will be ready to serve in 10 minutes," she tells me, readying herself to go back to the kitchen. Before she leaves, I reach for her wrist and grasp it gently, I feel her delicate muscles tense beneath my fingers. I want to tell her I mean no harm, but the words don't come out. The softness of her flesh between my palm snatches my words, so I go to what is on autopilot.

"Thank you, Victoire." She doesn't acknowledge me, instead, she waits for me to release my hold, and when I finally do, her wrist drops to her side and she rubs it against her dress. I watch as she disappears down the corridor, then I turn, and open my home to Jäger.

DINNER GUEST

At a well-dressed dining table
In a manor on the countryside
Three men watch a maid

Emil

This maggot sits at my table drinking my wine, feeding on my meat, all the while keeping a filthy eye on Victoire. Rolf and I sit at either end of the table, while Jäger sits in the middle, giving him a full view of her lovely curves, and red defined lips when she enters the room. She doesn't check on us, she remains in the kitchen tending to herself as we dine. His entire repertoire is boorish and loathsome as he recycles the same bits of debate and remarks overheard at Schröder's party, from his elation at the Führer's grand designs for Paris and the whole of Europe, to his interest in the rumored possibility of assisting the Italians in Northern Africa. Rolf leaves the table during this part. He is visibly shaken, though Jäger takes no notice. In fact, he's hardly turned to Rolf's side of the table all night, his elitist ancestry giving him confidence in his rude manner. Rolf goes to the kitchen to 'check on dessert'. He returns several minutes later with Victoire and her honey cake in tow. Jäger watches her carefully as she cuts the healthy slices.

"Where are you from?" he asks Victoire, his timber keen. She gives him a soft smile, keeping her brilliant white teeth a seductive secret.

"Paris."

"Born there?"

"Oui, Monsieur," she nods as she continues to cut the cake. She is graceful, serving me first, placing a dollop of cream on the side of my plate, then picking up a spoon, dipping it in a porcelain bowl full of honey and drizzling it over my portion, just as I like it. "Café, Herr von Konig?"

"Ou-"

"Where is your family from," he rudely interrupts my moment with Victoire, but she continues to serve me and finishes before she answers him.

"My Mother is from America, New Orleans, my Father too, by way of Haiti," she keeps her eyes focused on the task at hand.

"Interesting, the Haitians are very dark, your mother must have been–." Rolf, slams his hand on the table, rattling the cups and saucers, but Victoire counters his anger with softness.

"Café, Herr Bliss?" She pours, not waiting for his answer, "Shall I add some extra honey for your cake? This German coffee is strong but nothing a little sweetness can't handle." She smiles at Rolf knowingly, and her simple gesture calms him.

"My mother is Quadroon, Herr Jäger. Would you like a

dollop of cream with your cake," she asks as she continues her focused, long, graceful movements.

"Yes. I like cream...*plenty.*"

This. Fucking. Dog.

"Thank you, Victoire," is all I say, my eyes fixed on Jäger, his eyes fixed on Victoire. She picks up the cake and leaves the room. I grip my napkin so tightly my knuckles turn white.

Ten minutes later Rolf and I have gulped down our desserts, both playing the same games we played as boys, 'the faster you finish, the faster you can leave', except the one we want to leave is Jäger. However, Jäger is not through with his own game, puffing lightly on his thin cigar, leaning back in his chair, resting it on two legs. He's quiet for a moment, then sighs with a grin.

"This has been a most interesting evening von Konig," he declares, smiling coolly, watching the kitchen door. "You have a lovely home, well-appointed and certainly well taken care of, it warms my heart. Your mother and father will be happy to know you are being served well." I nod slowly and only once, acknowledging his veiled threat. "I wrote to *my* Vater about your living situation, and he was quite intrigued." I make no motion. "I wonder, has your maid any tips she could offer to my own? Mine seems to have trouble swallowing nuances of more detailed tasks like polishing, buffing, waxing and so forth. Perhaps your girl would be willing to extend her proficiencies to...*my* staff?" My jaw ticks at his innuendo, and I've had enough. I stand, my legs pushing my chair back with force, fire burning up my neck. Rolf makes a simple gesture with his hand for me to sit down, while he serenely stirs the remains of his coffee. "Easy von Konig," Jäger chuckles, shaking his head, "No need to be so tense." I take my cue from Rolf, "Shall we yawn in your den, a snifter of brandy perhaps, before I head home?" Jäger gets up from his seat and heads down the hall toward the den. I move swiftly to Rolf, livid with his calm demeanor when not just moments ago he was ready to kill.

"What the fuck is this, Rolf!?" I whisper loudly, mimicking his hand gesture. Rolf shakes his head slowly.

"He's baiting you. He wants a reason to go to your father, who you know holds your inheritance and your position here, in Paris and not in the belly of a fucking Panzer, in his hands," he snaps back, "Say you give him what he wants...then what? What happens to you then? To your practice, to Victoire? Finish the night. Let him walk out the door with a full belly and empty hands." I look down, tapping my finger on the table and contemplating my friend's words.

"Let's go."

Rolf gets up from the table and heads to the den. I b-line for the kitchen and open the door to see Victoire cleaning a few dishes. She doesn't look in my direction though she knows I'm here, she answers before I speak.

"Yes, Herr von Konig," her voice is tight but low, drawing me near her. I take a few strides to her side.

"Thank you for tonight Victoire, everything was wonderful." She continues to wash, still only focusing on the dishes. I wait for a response, but she gives none. "We take our leave to the den for the evening," I pause "anytime you choose, feel free to retire. We shall take care for ourselves the rest of the night." She continues in silence, I raise my hand from my side to touch her but think better of it and retreat through the door, down the corridor to the den.

Rolf is back to work on the bottle he started before dinner, on one side of the room, while Jäger rolls a snifter in his hand on the other looking over my books and records.

"Ah, I see you enjoy jazz," he places his drink on the bookshelf, pulling out a Louis Armstrong record, "Shall we?

Jungle music has always intrigued me." I begin to rush toward him as he turns to the record player, slipping the pressed vinyl from its sleeve. Before I can get past Rolf, he sticks his leg out from his flopped position in the club chair, hitting the front of my thighs. He shakes his head slowly. Satchmo's "Sweet as a Song" fills the room. Jäger snaps his fingers, offbeat, I almost laugh. Rolf doesn't even try to hide his grin.

"Where does one take a piss in this baby mansion of yours?"

"There is a small wash room around the corner on your left," I grit. He swallows the rest of his brandy and smiles.

"Thank you, three glasses of wine and two cups of coffee, I can't hold it anymore." He walks to the door looking left and right, then turns left out of sight." I drag myself to the kanapee, placing my head in my hands. I look at Rolf and roll my eyes.

"Scheiße! Panzer or no, I'm calling it a night as soon as this asshole gets back," I sigh.

Rolf smirks, "Agreed."

Victoire

ON MY WAY out of the kitchen to go to bed, I am stopped in the door by Herr Jäger. He is tall and handsome, but his eyes are like mirrors, only reflecting, allowing no admittance to his soul. His dark brown hair is disheveled and split down the middle, a cowlick that no amount of pomade could fix. He is lean and wiry, muscles coiled tightly around bone, a hidden, unexpected strength, like a snake who lays quietly waiting for a mouse to pass him three, four even five times before he strikes, crushing the mouse in his strong jaws in one gulp. I step backward into the kitchen; his body gives me no choice. I speak loudly hoping for Herr von Konig or Herr Bliss to hear me asking him if there was anything he needed, but the music in the den is too loud, Louie is singing about love, while I am staring down a jackal.

"Are you lost, Monsieur? Can I fetch Herr von Konig for you?" He doesn't answer me, he just keeps walking toward me until I am backed against a wall. I bring my arms up across my chest, clasping my wrists together, trying to see past him toward the door, praying that someone will come soon.

"You are lovely...for what you are," his staccato German accent sours in my ear. He traps me between his arms, pressing himself forward so his forehead leans against the wall right next to my ear. "I am curious to know what you look like under these aprons you wear, even though I shouldn't be," he drags his finger softly down my neck, "It's illegal you know, Rassenmischung, but your mother being a Quadroon, I guess the Führer could forgive me," he lowers one arm from the wall, and I take the opportunity to get away, but his next words stop me cold. "Or...I could make a visit...drop a hint...have your precious savior brought up on charges, shipped off to God knows where for years on end." A scowl sweeps across my face, I know he's not lying, I've heard the stories, I've had friends go missing while family members go on about their happy lives as if they'd never existed, a culture of tattletales, sending friends, family even the postman off to fates unknown. I can't let that happen to Herr von Konig. He saved my life, sheltered me, makes no demands, washes warmth over me with his ocean blue eyes. *No.* I try to call his bluff.

"There is nothing going on here, I am a maid," I say

harshly, pointing my finger as if that will stop his verbal advance.

"Isn't there," he steps forward, "I've watched you both closely all evening. He smiles, you shiver. You sigh, he imagines," he continues to advance, "You live here, the both of you alone, it would take no time for–"

"What do you want?"

He grins widely, a cat with feathers in his teeth.

"A tiny, little, kiss."

Emil

ROLF and I start laughing and drinking, and we don't notice that the song has changed until we hear a small crash coming from the back of the house. We look at each other wide eyed. It doesn't take anyone that long to piss, *FUCK!* I'm on my feet first, racing toward the kitchen. I fling open the door, and a split second later Rolf bumps into me. *What the fuck am I seeing?* Jäger is kissing down Victoire's neck. She sits on the small round kitchen table, her legs parted while Jäger stands between them, her hands gripping the edge of the table. A red mist forms and hovers. Jäger looks over to me and grins.

"Well, hello von Konig!" He then turns to Rolf and nods, "Neureich."

The mist descends…

Jäger, laughing.
    Red Mist.

Victoire against a wall.
    Red Mist.

Rolf blocking Jäger.
    Red Mist.

"Fuck you Neureich!"
    Red Mist.

My hands around Jäger's neck.
    Red Mist.

"Emil, NO! STOP! You'll kill him! STOP!"
    Red Mist.

"Herr von Konig, no!"
    The mist ascends…

I am in my den. Alone. Confused, and many bottles of whisky calling to me.

18

DRUNK

In the middle of a new room
At 2 a.m.
A woman encounters a beast

Victoire

Herr von Koning traps me between his arms, my back against the large window. I can't bring myself to look at him as the tears well in my eyes. He says nothing as he breathes into the darkness of my room. I can smell the alcohol on his breath, heavy and cloying. I can't stop the tears from coming, I just want to go back to bed.

"Herr von Konig," I cry softly.

"No!"

I jump at the booming timbre of his voice, it ricochets off my chest, accelerating my heartbeat. I look up, my face a twisted mess of tears. My vision adjusts to the darkness and pale moonlight as my gaze searches around him for some-thing, anything to anchor me besides his eyes. But his face tracks my every movement, not giving me the chance to focus on anything in particular. "Wipe off your lipstick," he commands softly. I hadn't noticed I still had it on, I came straight to my room, changed and buried myself under the covers, crying myself to sleep. I bring my trembling fingers to my lips. "Wipe! It! Off!" he yells at the top of his lungs only inches from my face. I don't move fast enough for him, so he grabs my head, cradling it in his large hands, roughly wiping my lips with his thumbs.

"Monsieur, please," I beg as he mushes my lips.

"Please," he mocks me, "Please, what?" I shake my head not knowing what to say as his thumbs work hard at removing every trace of color. "Is that what you wanted Victoire," again his voice is mocking and patronizing, "Hmm? Is that what you wanted my Angel? Is that what you painted your face for? Hmm, tell me? ANSWER ME!" I look around him, still searching, trembling.

"I didn't *want* anything!"

"No." He shakes his head, "Tell me the truth. Don't lie to me," his voice wavers, and for a moment he sounds like he's about to cry. I feel the heat from his body growing closer as he lowers his head just above the space between my neck and shoulder. He inhales deeply, "You didn't even bathe my Angel, I can still smell him on you?" I cringe at his harsh words and fight back another surge of tears. "Again, I will ask you, is that what you wanted? His hands up your dress, hmm? Did you let him touch you?"

"Stop. Please, Herr von Konig, you've had much to drink," I cry meekly, bringing my hands up to his chest pushing him back, but he's built like a wall of granite, my efforts are fruitless.

His demeanor softens, and there is an audible catch in his throat.

"Answer me," he whimpers, "Did you let him touch you, Angel? Why didn't you push at him like you're pushing me now," he sniffs along my hairline, landing a flurry of tiny wet butterfly-like kisses. "Angel, tell me," he begs me, desperately. Then suddenly the moment of tenderness is gone and he lowers his face, pressing his nose against mine. "Five months my Angel," he grits out, his voice deep and gruff "five months, we've said no more than five words to each other, yet in five minutes you had a stranger's hand fingering your hot little pussy, didn't you?"

Heat shoots up my backbone and I push hard enough to move him from my face, "Don't speak to me that way!" In the moonlight, I can see the color of his face grow a shade darker, with a grim look of incredulity.

"I will speak to you any way I wish Angel," more mocking, "shall I whisper filthy things in your ear like our guest?"

"Don't." I push at his chest again, bringing my knees up and striking them against his thighs in a fury, but he presses his body between my legs, the windowsill digs into my bottom. I move my head from side to side, up and down trying to keep his mouth from my ear, his breathy pants of exertion hitting me each way I turn.

"No, no, no Angel, listen-listen-listen, shhhhhh. Don't you want to hear what filthy little things I have to say, hmm? They are my secrets, so I must whisper them to you, ja!?" He grabs the back of my neck instantly stopping my head from turning away. He brings his other hand to my waist gripping me so tight it hurts, his large hands like boa constrictors, holding me to him. I hate that it hurts...so good. I hate that his rough, drunken touch is making me wet. I will my body not to respond to his massive frame between my legs, his stiff member pushed against my stomach. I will my hips not to rock into him. Herr von Konig's grip on my waist opens. His hand glides up my body softly. His thumb makes small circles around my belly button then glides up to my breast making more tiny circles, *God help me*. From my breast, he moves to my face caressing it, then over to my neck where he tips my head back against the window locking me between his hands. Tears roll down from my eyes, over my ears, and down my back. My hands grip the sides of the window. I want to reach out and touch him, hold him, wrap my legs around his waist and tell him what he saw isn't what he thinks.

I make a final plea, "Monsieur, please, let me go."

"Nein, nein, nein, hör' zu. Mein Engel, ich möchte dich vor mich hinlegen und deine Muschi schön langsam essen. An deinem hübschen kleinen Kitzler saugen, bis ich deine Creme auf meiner Zunge spüre. Ich möchte der Mann sein, der dich befriedigt wie kein anderer zuvor. Ich möchte, dass du mich reitest. Ich möchte sehen, wie deine Augen in deinen Kopf zurückrollen, während du auf meinen fetten Schwanz spritzt. Ich werde dich für jeden anderen Mann ruinieren, deine Muschi wird keine andere Wahl haben, als nach mir zu verlangen," [*No, no, no, listen. My Angel, I want to lay you down in front of me and eat your pussy nice and slow. Suck on your pretty little clit until I feel your cream on my tongue. I want to be the man who will satisfy you like no other before. I want you to ride me I want to see your eyes roll back into your head as you cum on my fat cock. I will ruin you for any other man, your pussy will have no choice but to crave for me,*] he reaches down and pulls my leg around his waist bringing my heat in direct contact with his member. I know he can feel me. He lets out a slow, sinister laugh, then licks the shell of my ear. He sways his hips side to side brushing against my clit, and we stare at each other longingly for what seems an eternity as he rocks me, like a baby. His eyes mist and he returns to my ear.

"Du bist mein Engel, als er dich berührt hat, hast du mich beinahe zerrissen. Wie konntest du dich von ihm berühren lassen, Baby?" [*You are my Angel, when he touched you, you almost tore me apart. How could you let him touch you, Baby?*] he trails more warm butterfly kisses up my ear, as his thumb makes languid circles at the side of my neck. "Warum hast du nicht nach mir gerufen? Sag mir, dass du ihn nicht wolltest," [*Why didn't you call for me? Tell me you didn't want him,*] his voice wavers again, his sniffling giving me a deeper clue to what he's feeling, though I don't understand the words, and just as I thought his anger subsided, something clicks and he changes, closing the grip on my neck tighter. I almost cum. "SAG ES MIR! Ich will dich. Ich wollte dich seit der Nacht, in der ich dich das erste Mal gesehen habe, Victoire," [*TELL ME! I want you. I've wanted you since the night I first saw you, Victoire*] he growls in my ear. "Shall I translate for you my Angel?"

"No! Get out!" He grips my neck even tighter, snatching me to him. I squeal and scratch at his hands and wrists, I can see darkness closing in at my periphery, my lungs start to burn.

He chuckles low in my ear, "Nevermind, I'll just show you." His hands leave my neck and he moves back, releasing me. I hop up from the windowsill and try to quickly sidestep him. He grabs my wrist. I snatch it away, but he pulls me into his chest and begins to savagely kiss and lick my shoulders and neck.

"Arrête ça!" [*Stop it!*] I shout. His tongue continues its assault. His inebriation amplifies his anger...his agony. I didn't want that man, Jäger to touch me. However, I don't know how to tell him the things he said about how he could have Herr von Konig brought up on charges for "Rassenmischung", *miscegenation.* "Consorting with an inferior race," he said, all while inching his hand inside my dress. I wanted to scream, to yell for Herr von Konig to come save me from that pig of a man, but how could I, how could I send the man I am slowly and totally falling in love with to such a fate as prison or worse? I made a decision, which was to keep my mouth shut and let it be done. At that very moment, Herr von Konig and Herr Bliss burst into the kitchen.

The look on Herr von Konig's face was incomprehensible. But, rage soon took over, and he flew at Jäger, ripping him away from me by his collar, the force of his anger frightened me so. I fell to the floor and backed up against the wall in fear. Poor Herr Bliss a bundle of nerves, not knowing whether to come to my aide or stop Herr von Koning from bashing in Jäger's face. I screamed for Herr von Koning to stop, starting Herr Bliss in his direction. He ran in between them, yelling for the commotion to end. Jäger only smiled and laughed, just waiting for a punch to land. I stood on my shaky legs making my way to Herr von Konig's side. I pulled on his steel arm, tensed and drawn back. The look he gave me sent chills through my body. I immediately removed my hands and ran to my room. I could hear their boots scuffling about, leaving the kitchen, then there was the slamming of the door. Hours passed as I cried, buried beneath my covers. I got up to use the bathroom, and when I returned to bed Herr von Konig was standing in the middle of my room, bottle in hand.

Now, here he is, drunk and handling me roughly, whispering things in German I don't understand. His hand squeezes my breast so hard the pain is almost intolerable.

"I can smell you Victoire, did you let him sniff your pussy, did-he-get-a-taste!?" he spits out venomously.

After all I have allowed him to say. As rough as I have allowed him to handle me, this was enough. I am done.

"Emil, ENOUGH!"

SLAP!

I bring my hand across the side of his face as hard as I am able.

SLAP!

I strike his face again.

His head is turned in the direction of my blows. The only sound is our tandem breathing, hard, and stuttering. He releases his grip, keeping his head turned as he picks up the bottle he set down on my nightstand, then walks to the door.

"Emil," I try to say sternly, but my voice shakes. My hands wring at the material of my cotton nightgown. He stops at the threshold, his hand gripping the top of the door so tightly I hear the squeaking of the wood. "Don't you ever touch me like that again. Do you understand," I say as strongly as I can between tears and gritted teeth.

"Hmpf," he chuckles, shaking his head, "Did you give *him* the same admonishment," he asks pointedly. "Not to worry mein Engel," he takes a swig from his bottle still looking ahead, "should I ever have the pleasure of touching you again, it will be, most certainly, upon your request...not one verdammnt [*damned*] moment before." He tosses the bottle on my floor, splashing liquor all around, the lead crystal only chipping slightly, then rolling to a stop.

"Emil!" I call to him. He slams the door behind him, leaving me alone when I need him most. I wrap my arms around my middle tightly and slip to the floor, drowning in my own tears.

19

VERBAL ONSLAUGHT

In a blue bedroom
Of a quiet house
A man searches for paper

THE HOME OF HERR VON KONIG

Emil

I'm too ashamed to face Victoire this morning. My drunken madness led me to her room last night where I nearly broke her. After witnessing her in the kitchen with Jäger's hands and lips all over her body, I lost it. My anger was misdirected, but it nearly drove me mad to see her allowing him to touch her...taste her. It wasn't but the night before she was calling for me in her sleep to satisfy her. My intent was to go to her and apologize for what had happened, but I realized that I wasn't sure what happened. Was she enjoying it? Had she seduced him? Had he taken advantage of her? Rage filled me and I began to drink to calm my head, but it did the opposite. I nearly choked my Angel, desperate for her to tell me she didn't want him.

I pull out a piece of paper from my writing desk in the corner of my room. I sit and stare out the window into the cold, grey morning for a moment, thinking of what to say, then I begin my letter. I know it's not enough, but until I can clear my head and rally my courage to face her, it will have to do.

Victoire

I LIE in bed gently rubbing my neck. He left no bruises, there is no physical pain, only the pain from knowing that what I allowed Jäger to do tempted a beast. Emil. Who is this man? Do I really know him, have I ever known him? From the day he brought me here he has been somber, patient...kind. Yesterday morning when he touched me, I nearly melted in his hands, hands I have craved to hold me and caress me since the moment he told me his name. But last night a lion awoke from its slumber and its rage was directed fully, toward me. I was only trying to protect him, that's all I wanted to do...but how could I tell him this?

I don't want to see him this morning. This morning he will make his own way for breakfast and lunch. This morning I will lay here in my new warm bed by the fire and wait to hear his footsteps out the front door.

As I close my eyes to try and fall back asleep, a light wisping noise comes through my door. I turn over but see nothing, my new bed is too large and too full of beautiful blankets and pillows to accomplish much by way of seeing. I slip from under the covers, put on my robe and go to the door where I see Herr von Konig has slipped an envelope with my name written on it. As I pull it from under the door, I hear a car horn and the front door slam. Herr Bliss must have decided to make another trip to collect his friend, no doubt to discuss the night's happenings. *Good.* I think today I will take a drive over to my cottage. I head to my closet to look for something to wear. I pull out a simple black and white silk dress, with a matching hat and gloves and a black velvet purse. *I think I'll hot comb my hair and pin it.* I shove the letter in my purse, not yet wanting to deal with its contents, then head to the bathroom to have a bath. I want to wash the night away, then have a day to myself.

Emil

THE WHOLE RIDE TO PARIS, Rolf has been silent. It's almost deafening. I know he is thinking about how to confront me about last night. He told me not to do it, he even begged me to let him take Victoire back with him to the city, but Victoire declined bitterly. I ultimately decided it was best for her to stay, *who am I kidding*, I wanted her to stay with me, no one else. If I am honest with myself, I am a jealous of the rapport that Rolf has with Victoire. They had an almost instant connection, like old friends. He calls for her and asks after her, he even makes her laugh, something I have yet to do.

We round the corner and stop in front of my office. Rolf thanks his man then exits the car at the same time as I do.

"Shall we take a stroll around the block?" he asks looking at his watch, "You have some time before your patients arrive don't you?" I nod, keeping silent, allowing my friend to collect his thoughts. We drift aimlessly through the streets, strolling past a small park, where some elderly French men play chess under watch of a few soldiers. I hear Rolf taking the morning air into his lungs, breathing deeply, his eyes closed, face toward the cold overcast sun.

We make our way back toward my office, about a block away is when Rolf finally comes to life. He turns sharply, standing his tall, lean body directly in front of me. His eyes are sunken and dark, a telltale sign of his drinking binges and lack of sleep.

"The shite you pulled last night could land us both in dire straights," he hisses coolly, keeping his voice low, "Do you think you are the only one who has dipped his tongue in black treacle?" My eyes widen in bewilderment. "No my friend. I myself have found that the sweetest cunts in all the world belong to women many shades darker than you and me, but where you go wrong, Emil, is to announce your enthusiasm at a time like this!" I take a step forward ready to fight my friend of 30 years, but he doesn't back down.

"What are you saying?" I growl through gritted teeth. Rolf matches my stance, then suddenly, without warning, he shoves my back against a parked car, his forearm sinking into my throat. I've never known my friend to be violent or easily provoked, thus I had no idea that his strength matched, even surpassed, my own. The grimace on his face only enhances his ire, "I am saying she's beautiful, and they are jealous of your money, and vanity station. Calm yourself, and stop letting your emotions speak for you–they will only use them to their advantage!"

Rolf releases his forearm from my neck with a push and backs away from me so that I might remove myself from the car door in which he slammed me, he looks around, nodding to fellow officers and onlookers with a Cheshire cat grin.

I rub my throat, immediately thinking of Victoire and how her throat must feel this morning. Pangs of hurt and guilt course through me, *I will never touch her that way again.*

"I--I haven't tasted her, or any other woman like her before," I stutter out in a compound of embarrassment and shame. Rolf turns on his heel giving me only a view of his profile.

"Then, I haven't ruined the surprise for you," he states, stiffening his shoulders, and rolling his neck to a crack. His voice is low, just above a whisper, "I know what it is to love and not be able to show it...hiding something decadent and bright in corners and dark rooms. This–this world, this train we are on is diseased, the very same disease that has propelled us into this war that you nor I can escape. I don't plan to hide when this is over, and I'll do my damndest to keep my hands clean until then, however long it takes. Even if that means working under my Vater's orders riding a desk at Intelligence, and kissing the most disgusting backward pig arses known to man...because when this is done," he swirls his hand around in the air flippantly, "I have my own business to attend to."

My friend is silent for a long moment, even reverent. Then, like someone flipping on a switch, he returns to his fractionated self, the cupped version of Rolf I have come to know these many months since Marrakech; the sad humorist, a brooding, *faux* playboy wearing a shroud of acute charm. He spins to face me again, his grin returning, "I am your brother, for all intents and purposes. I will keep you safe. We both know your pansy arse would never make it anywhere without me managing your fists, ja?" He slaps my shoulder heavily, his full, hearty laugh earning smiles from the pale blonde Fräuleins that walk by, and a few tips of the cap from officers and businessmen. He looks into my eyes and there is an intensity, a despondency that continues to grow. They speak of a woman who must be like Victoire, no wonder he is so taken with her, she must be his only emotional connection to whomever his heart is aching for. Once again, I feel pangs of guilt. I nod to him in acknowledgment. He clicks his heels and salutes me, then whispers in my ear "FICK,Heil, " his eyebrows raise up and down like Groucho Marx, then he walks away. "I shall pick you up today at 4:30 my friend," he calls behind, sauntering down the sidewalk in his natural debonair style, "Finish your work and be ready to go." He goes back to enjoying the cold morning air.

ROLF

On a hot night
In a beautiful seaside villa
A woman hums

A PRIVATE BEACH ON THE MORROCAN COAST | AUGUST 1939

Rolf

I open the slatted doors leading out to the deck and inhale deeply. The air smells of salt water, and the night sky looks down on me with bright beaming stars. I can't stop smiling as I listen for Ayouba. This is what life should be, a man alone in his own home, with a woman he loves listening to her hum sweetly throughout the house. I bought this villa just for Ayouba and me. I promised her father that I would keep her safe wherever we were.

"Mia figlia è nera," Ayouba's father said to me one day, out of the blue, while we cataloged a few of his artifacts. "I know you two are in love. However, there will come a day that brings trouble, just like there was for Ayouba's mother and me. I fought for her mother fiercely. Ayouba is my bambina. She is precious and deserving of every good thing. This world will try and make her feel that she is not, just because my bambina has skin that is opulenta [*opulent*], and unrivaled. Prove to me that I am letting her keep company with a man that will protect her just as fiercely and recognizes her beauty." To prove that, I purchased a private villa near the beach, and I've told no one about it, not even Emil. With the impending war and people's sentiments about culture more sour than ever, I want Ayouba as quietly kept as possible.

It has been two years now since I first met her. I came to Marrakech tracking down an Ottoman dagger I was outbid for in Sicily. I figured I could find the buyer and offer him a price. What I didn't expect was for the buyer, a rather broad and intimidating Italian, to be the father of the most exquisite piece of art I had ever seen. In all my travels, I had never come across a woman as magnificent as Ayouba. Ayouba's father traveled to Ethiopia in hopes to claim a piece of land for himself and instead fell in love with her mother, a beautiful, Ethiopian woman with eyes like a cupie doll. There was nowhere for them to live in Ethiopia or Italy, so they settled on Morocco on the coast, living a quiet, happy life, raising three children: two boys and Ayouba.

I emerge from my thoughts, wondering where she could be as the sound of her humming has silenced. When I turn to re-enter the house I see her. I don't care how many times I see her, my body has the same reaction. I am rigid from the bottom of my feet to the top of my head and everywhere in between. Ayouba is walking toward me naked as a jaybird. Her hair is an amazing inky black woolen mass of coils shooting in all directions, hitting her shoulders, rooted to her russet brown skin. Her height, she takes from her father, making her an exceptionally formidable opponent in bed. Her long strong legs grip my waist just right, but damn if her curves don't come from her mother.

"Habibta. aljaw har," [*My love. It's hot.*] she sings to me as she walks past switching her swollen hips, making her ass jiggle; she knows it drives me crazy. Before she passes me completely, she shoots back her hand placing it under my chin, scratching me like a little puppy.

"Soggezione, è vero. Il mio piccolo Austriaco non parla Arabo. Un giorno dovrò insegnartelo. Adesso vieni, ho caldo e voglio nuotare con te," [*Awe, that's right! My little Austrian doesn't speak Arabic. Someday I'll have to teach you. Come now, I'm hot and I want to swim with you*] she laughs, dropping her hand from my chin then waving me to come on, "stai sbavando, asciugati la saliva prima di scivolarci sopra!!" [*you're drooling you should wipe it up before you slip!*]

My eyes grow large from her teasing. She sees I'm about to pounce, which makes her double over with laughter before running from me at top speed screaming. She's headed toward our little private strip of beach. I quickly run inside to the divan, ripping off a blanket, then make my way after Ayouba at breakneck speed. I was track captain in finishing school in England, Ayouba doesn't stand a chance. She looks back and screams again. I'm two steps from her, I reach out grabbing her waist. I pull her to me and spin her around, delighting in the feel of her hair against my face. I toss the blanket on the sand then start making my way to the water, Ayouba is squealing trying to wiggle her way out of my grasp.

"No! No, Amore! No!" she laughs and squeaks.

"Sì, Ayouba! Mi prendi in giro fin troppo! Hai detto che eri calda, adesso ci penso io a te," [*Yes, Ayouba! You make fun of me too much! You said you were hot, now I'm gonna take care of you*] I laugh and growl in her ear. The water is at my feet, nice and cool, I run in and splash Ayouba and I both under the water, still with a tight grasp around her waist. Seconds later Ayouba breaks the water's surface, her hair covering her face.

"Aaaaaaahh! Stronzo!" Her fists fly at my chest and arms and I laugh so hard I almost pee! I wrap my arms around her tighter, stopping her assault. With one hand, I brush her hair up and over, revealing her face. Dark mahogany eyes sparkle above a set of cherubic cheeks. I glide my other hand down her back and cup her voluminous ass cheek pulling her up and on my waist, she rocks her hips slightly into me and I lose all restraint. I capture her lips, kissing her hungrily, my tongue exploring every inch of her mouth, feasting on her moans. She struggles to gain control, but I won't let her, I suck her tongue into my mouth; it drives her wild. Ayouba reaches down in the water, spreading her legs wide rubbing her clit up and down against my clothed cock. She arches back in pleasure and I take advantage, bending over and claiming a pebbled espresso bud in my mouth. I nibble and lick, keeping my eyes on her, watching her please herself. I push her back from me and place both my hands under her ass, allowing her to float.

"Rolf," she whimpers.

"Muovi le braccia, piccola," [*Move your arms, baby*] she moves her arms gracefully through the water to help keep herself afloat, "Non importa cosa succede, non fermarti." [*No matter what happens, don't stop.*] I sink down in the water to bring myself just above level with her pussy, draping her legs over my shoulders. I take two fingers and place them gently between her puffy lips and caress up and down the sides of her slickened pearl, her breath hitches and she trembles in my hands.

"Hai un sapore così dolce," [*You taste so sweet*] I whisper to her just before I draw her clit into my mouth. I moan at the burst of flavor on my tongue. I pull back for a moment to gather my senses then dive in again, this time sucking in her entire mound. I'm so hungry I make indelicate noises as I consume her, watching her heaving breasts rise and fall. I wrap my arm under her waist to help keep her afloat, then reach my other arm up to her ample breasts. I find a bud and roll it between my fingers, then I pinch it, hard. Ayouba jerks beneath me.

"Aah, Habibi, iyeh!" [*Aah, my love, yes*] I devour and slurp right through her first orgasm. I gorge myself, refusing to let up for a single second, even when she begins to kick at me, trying to push away, "La! Rolf, ti prego, così è troppo." [*No! Rolf, please, it's too much*]

I pull back and lick my lips, my breathing is heavy and my need for Ayouba is intense. I pull her to me, grabbing the back of her hair. A small whimper escapes her lips and I simper, biting my bottom lip, rocking her in my arms. I pull off my trousers, giving them to the sea, and in one smooth motion, I lift Ayouba and bring her down slowly on my cock. Ayouba says nothing, only leans forward pressing her forehead to mine, grabbing and tugging my hair roughly. Her mouth open, panting heavily. I hold her down on me tightly, indulging in the feel of her hips making methodical grinding and bouncing movements. I, on the other hand, can't shut up, letting every filthy utterance of my mother tongue fly through the air.

"Scheiße, Ayoubaaa! Deine Muschi ist so verdammt eng, Baby. Scheiße, du wurdest gemacht, um auf meinem Schwanz zu sitzen. Scheiße!" [*Shit, Ayboubaaa! Your pussy is so damn tight, Baby. Damn, you were meant to sit on my dick. Fuck!*] I turn us and walk out of the water to the blanket I threw to the sand moments ago. I lower to my knees gingerly, still buried deep inside my beautiful Ayouba. I release my grip around her waist, placing both of my hands on her hips as I begin to furiously rebound her up and down. Ayouba lands her feet flat in the blanket and takes over, grabbing the back of my neck and pulling me to nestle my head in the bend of throat, where I bite and kiss her. I can't control the moans that escape me. I slap her ass cheek with a giant huff, pull her off my cock then spin her around positioning her on her side. I move in behind her, marveling at the sway in her back that offers her posterior to me like a gift. I rub it, feeling her push back on my pelvis. I chuckle then lift her leg, slipping inch by inch into her heat. The pace of my entry finally breaks Ayouba's silence.

"Oh, sì, sì, sì! Rolf!"

Her cries of pleasure are an erotic drug, I bang into her hard, placing two fingers over her clit, rubbing feverishly. My free arm cradles her, giving me access to her breasts, my thumb strumming, like a guitar, a tune of love over each stiffened nipple. She writhes in pleasure, whipping her arm around the back of my neck to lock me to her. Her sheath is hot and clenching, snatching, begging for my release. I feel the fire rising in my chest, then at the base of my spine. I lean my head against the back of Ayouba's neck and nip her.

"Cazzo!" she cries out to me.

I'm there, but I need her to be too, I want us to cum together. I pull my fingers from her sensitive bundle of nerves and place her on all fours without missing a single stroke. I slap the sweet brown skin of her ass again, thrusting hard.

"Sto per venire. Piccola ti voglio aspettare, non metterci troppo," [*I'm going to cum but I'm waiting for you. Baby don't make me wait*] I slap once more taking immense plea-sure in watching her bronze cheeks jiggle on my dick, "Ayou-ba!" I command.

"Sì, daddy! Ci sono quasi! Sto venendo!", [*Yes, daddy! Almost there! I'm coming!*] she whines to me in a husky voice.

Fuck, she called me 'Daddy.' I'm gonna cum so fucking hard.

Just as I feel Ayouba's walls clench around me, pulsing and yanking me, I let go of everything that has been welling up in my jewels. Long, thick ropes of my seed shoot deep into Ayouba. She spreads her legs wider on instinct as she takes in all I give to her. My chest is burning, and my hand somehow made its way back to Ayouba's hair, softly pulling and massaging. I raise my other hand to her hip, guiding her back and forth as she finishes her own release. Her arms give way and we fall forward on the blanket. I roll to my back and pull Ayouba to me, kissing the back of her neck, her shoul-ders, and down her spine. I swivel her head toward mine so I can take her mouth again. We moan in tandem at the taste of each other.

"Ti amo Ayouba, ti amo tanto." [*I love you Ayouba, I love you so much.*] I whisper in her ear, rubbing my nose against her cheek.

"Ti amo anche io Rolf, di più." [*I love you too Rolf, more.*]

∾

In a master bedroom
Overlooking the ocean

A PRIVATE BEACH ON THE MORROCAN COAST | NOVEMBER 1939

Rolf

"ROLF! AAUUUHH! AAAAUUH!" Ayouba screams out for the third time that I've made her cum on my tongue. I move up her body slowly to kiss her, "Mmm," she moans at the taste of her own juices on my lips.

"Rolf…"

"Si, amore." Ayouba hesitates for a few moments so I sit up on my elbow and wait for her to collect her thoughts. She gets up from the bed, pulling the sheet along with her, wrapping it around her body. My heart begins to beat a little faster. Ayouba never has trouble speaking to me or telling me what is exactly on her mind. She moves to stand in front of the doors that open to the balcony of our bedroom, leaning there…staring at me with a longing in her eyes. I move to the edge of the bed placing my feet on the floor preparing myself for what she has to say. *Please, Piccola don't leave me, anything but that.*

"Ayouba, speak to me, please." At my plea Ayouba's eyes glisten in the moonlight, I'm swiftly on my feet, my hands flying to cradle her beautiful face, "Speak to me Amore, please."

"Sono incinta." [*I'm pregnant.*]

I hesitate for a single moment, and Ayouba is away from me in a flash, running into the bedroom, pulling her clothes from the closets.

"Ayouba! Stop! What are you doing, Piccola! Please,

stop!" I pull her to me as she tries to fight past me to yank more of her clothes from the closest, crying inconsolably.

"La! Cretino--Stronzo! [*No! Cretin--Asshole!*] I knew I shouldn't have told you; I knew you wouldn't want us!"

Rage courses through my body. Is this what she truly thinks? I spin her to me and shake her.

"Amore! Amore! Listen to me. STOP!" I kiss her mouth with fervor though she tries to fight me off, I don't stop. I let my lips tell her what my heart feels. I kiss down her neck and shoulders, her arms and hands, soon I am on my hands and knees kissing her feet. I look up to her, feeling a knot forming in my throat that makes it hard for me to speak. My eyes begin to burn as tears form at the corners. I am *beyond* happy. "Amore mio, please, please listen. Piccola, I am without words. There is nothing that I can possibly say to express how overjoyed I am to know that you are carrying our child," my words begin to choke as my tears flow heavily from my eyes, I struggle to finish, "I--I...I have wanted a family of my own for so long, and when you came into my life Ayouba, I knew I wanted that with you. I love you Ayouba, I want you and our baby." I pull my gold signet ring from my pinky and slip it on her finger, turning the 'B' inward toward her heart, "This isn't the ring you deserve. Believe me, I had plans to get you one as large as my love for you, so large you'd probably have to tie your arm over your shoulder," we both laugh, "but right now, please accept this as my promise of love for you and our baby. Marry me Ayouba, say yes and seal this hole you have filled in my heart."

Ayouba falls to her knees and we stare at each other.

"Si, Amore."

"Ja!?'" I kiss her and hold her. This woman is my only reason to breathe, and now she is giving me a child, a chance to do all the wonderful things my father never did with me in his selfish pursuit of money. This baby will grow up without scorn or shame, a Bliss that can be proud. I place my hand on her belly, "How far along?" I rub back and forth in awe.

"Quasi due mesi," [*Almost two months,*] she coos with a bright smile.

"Amore," I cry and kiss her again, letting my tongue write our names along the walls of the warm cavern of her mouth. I am the happiest man alive.

Two blocks away from a pink cocktail lounge
On cloud nine

MARRAKECH | NOVEMBER 1939

Rolf

I'M drunk and so fucking happy, as I stroll down the street. I look down at my pinky finger where the signet ring my father gave me at my graduation used to be. This morning Ayouba and I went to her father and mother to ask her hand in marriage and to tell them we were pregnant. I was a little afraid at first, but her father and mother were elated. Carlo and I spoke about a proper ring for his daughter, he knows many fine jewelers and this following week we will travel to Bombay to purchase a diamond. I've been celebrating with him and her brothers all day long so I'm pretty much drunk, and in need of sleep...next to my fiancée, but I've been neglecting Emil since we've been here, sneaking off most days and nights to be with Ayouba. I feel guilty not asking my very best friend in the world to join me in our home, but I need to be sure it's safe, and I need to find a way to tell him about my double life. I want him to stand with me at my wedding, so I need to make it soon, then I will deal with my parents. I was pissed as fuck when my mother wrote me that the twin titties were already enroute to Marrakech to "keep us company", they're staying in the same hotel as Emil and I and it's been a pain to dodge Dottie. I look at my watch and pick up the pace, I was supposed to meet them 30 minutes ago. I pass by a small shop window and see a little silver baby rattle with intricate designs etched into the handle. It's late, and the shop is closed, but I'll come back tomorrow to purchase it. Ayouba will think it's ridiculous, but I don't care, our baby will have everything money can buy, and more love than anyone in the world.

I walk into the club and see my friend in the embrace of Lottie Schneagle, as usual, her tits are shoved in his grinning face. Dottie is even trying it on with him, but as a good friend should, he refuses her, *not that I care,* I laugh to myself. I stop at the bar and order two bottles of champagne. I loosen my tie and place the bottles under my dinner jacket. I want to continue the celebration, I'm on top of the world.

21

YOU CAN'T GO HOME AGAIN

At a manor on the countryside
On a cold morning
A car sits empty

THE HOME OF HERR VON KONIG | NOVEMBER
1940

Victoire

Herr von Konig never takes the keys to the car with him on the occasions he rides to work with Herr Bliss. I'm not certain as to why, but I always know where they are. When Herr von Konig comes home he tosses them in a little bowl on a table beside the bench in the vestibule.

I run my fingers over my hair, gently pressing a few loose bobby pins back in place. It took me almost three hours to hot comb and pin it up into two smart rolls, with a thick under curl. I look at my watch, *11:30*, if it were any other morning

I'd say the day is gone. But it's not, it's the morning after last night, a night I don't know how to feel about. So, instead of feeling anything, I shove it all aside, grab my coat, the keys and step out into the cold morning air. I breathe deeply, but it's too cold for me and I cough, trying to catch my breath. The car takes several turns for the engine to start, wheezing and clicking, then finally roaring to life. I pull out of the round driveway and take a right onto the empty black road; I know my cottage is only a few kilometers away. Herr Bliss and I have talked about it. He and Herr von Konig went and packed bags for me the day they brought me to the country-side. Herr Bliss is so kind as to give me updates and have his man stop by to check on the place for me from time to time. He has really been a true gentleman, and I would say that Herr von Konig is lucky to have him as a close friend. They balance each other.

As I think about the two men that currently occupy my life, I notice familiar tree patterns out of the window and I smile to myself, excited to see my cottage again. My excite-ment is halted when I hit, what must be, a series of rocks. I hear a tire pop, and the sound of gravel starts to grow louder in my ears as the car fishtails. I struggle to keep it on the road, but I manage to slow down and straighten the swiveling ton of metal, coming to a safe stop at the tree line.

"Fils de Pute!," [*Son of a bitch!*] I shout at the car ceiling, letting my back hit the seat and my arms flop down to my side. For a moment I'm silent, taking in the gravity of the past few moments, letting my heart return to its normal beat. With a large sigh, I get up and start to move. Wrapping my coat tight around my waist and neck, I grab my purse and shove it under my arm then stomp my way up the side of the country road, it's only a kilometer or two, but it's cold and dreary. By the time I come upon my cottage I am freezing to the bone.

The moment I step through the door I head straight to the fireplace. There is a small stack of wood and a gold bucket with kindling sitting on the hearth. I clap my hands together and close my eyes in silent prayer.

"Thank you, Jesus. Thank you, God! Oh, Herr Bliss, I could kiss you!" Once done with my prayer I go about starting the fire, the whooshing and crackling sounds are a happy welcome. The glowing blaze gives extra light to my cream and pink walls. I walk around touching and fluffing and fixing. My stomach growls, so I head toward the kitchen and open the pantry to find the canned goods that I had purchased months ago in preparation for me and my family's retreat from Paris. I pull out cans of asperges blanches [*white asparagu*s], and huile d'olive [*olive oil*]. I arch my brow comparing how much I would now have to pay on the black market for this single can of oil compared to the several cans that I have gone through while working for Herr von Konig. His station and family money no doubt has allotted for the many roasts and honey cakes I have made for him over the months, also living in the countryside doesn't hurt.

There are many times I've traded my bread or can of oil for meat, cream, and butter. With Herr von Konig's avid permission, I started a small garden that quickly yielded us a few small but beautiful vegetables over the summer. I giggle to myself remembering the morning I left out a little basket full of vegetables for my little friend in the woods, it sat for two whole days before it finally disappeared, the need to keep him healthy with good greens and colors of the garden compelled me to withhold milk, jam and bread until the basket was gone, then of course like any good mother, I left my Little Rabbit a full loaf of bread, lashings of butter and two giant slices of honey cake. *Mother.* Herr von Konig's eyes jumped in surprise late one evening when he sneaked into the kitchen to cut himself a slice and it was almost half gone. I wasn't sure I should tell him about my Little Rabbit in the woods so I took the blame on myself, he stared at me for a moment, raking his eyes over my hips, then with his signature smirk, cut himself a slice and retreated somewhere within the house.

I search the drawers for a can opener, find it and place it on the small counter, then I reach up and pull a saucepan down from the rack. My stomach growls again.

"Alright," I whisper to it in frustration, then remember the small piece of bread I wrapped quickly and threw in my purse, just in case there was no food here, I couldn't remember what I had or hadn't stashed away. I cross from the kitchen through the pink sitting room, to the green crushed velvet settee, which I purchased for the purpose of lying right under this particular window so the sun could wash over my face during the day. I eye my purse and grab it as another growl rolls through my stomach. I open it to look for the bread, instead I see the letter Herr von Konig slipped under my door. I wait to eat my bread, choosing to fill my mind instead of my belly. With a great sigh, I open the envelope and pull out the neatly folded letter—

Dearest Victoire,

My father and this war have made me a coward. In all of my bravado and stature, I find myself easily succumbing to powers that overwhelm me. My anger, a product of my youth, has only grown more emboldened with the weakening of my spirit. Yet and still this is no excuse for how I treated you last night. My only intentions were to come to you and see to your safety and rest, but I waited too long, nervous about what you thought of my actions with Jäger. I couldn't be sure if what I saw was real, and it ripped me apart. To see another man touching you gnawed at me mercilessly until I had finished a bottle of whisky and had gone back for more. My hands have always been my prized possessions, from boxing to being a surgeon, but I promise you I would cut them off before I ever harm you again.

Should you ever allow me to touch you again, it will be by your request alone and not before, I must earn this right.

Please forgive me Victoire, please.

With all my heart,

Emil

I fold the note, placing it back in its envelope, staring ahead somewhere down the hall of my empty cottage. My stomach, that just moments ago was growling with hunger, is now silent and twisted in large tightly wound knots. I feel the sting of tears welling up in my eyes, but for what? Anger? Pity? Sadness? Relief? I don't know. I'm confused and over-whelmed.

'Please forgive me Victoire, please. With all my heart, Emil.'

I need to lie down for a moment. A slight shiver runs through me even with the fire. I fetch a blanket from my room and lay down on the settee to think. My eyes become heavy, and before I know what has happened, I drift off into a fitful sleep.

I JUMP at the sound of car doors slamming. It takes me a moment to remember where I am, *no one knows I'm here*, I push off the blanket, and look at the fire which has died out. I must have been asleep for hours, I look at my watch, *4 o'clock.* The sun is already beginning to set.

"Merde," I whisper to myself, then hear another car door, I turn slowly to the window to investigate the sound and my eyes grow wide with fear. Through my window, I count two black cars and 1 green utility vehicle. A small but hard looking band of soldiers emerge, slamming their doors. There is one last door that opens at the back of the furthest black car, *Jäger!*

They approach the cottage slowly, looking around the grounds and trying to peer through the windows, I grab my purse and slam my body to the floor. Fear of discovery is making my limbs heavy, and I'm unable to move, like when trying to run in a dream and your legs feel like weights marred down in sludge. I try to hold my breath. I swear they can hear me breathing through the door, but my heart is racing too fast and I begin to hiccup for lack of oxygen. *I can't stay here on the floor*, I hear their footsteps on the gravel growing closer, then I hear the door handle begin to twist, *did I lock it, Oh please God, tell me I locked it?* Instead of waiting for the answer for if I locked it, I obey His command to move. Flipping off my shoes and holding them in the crooks of my fingers, I grab my purse and crawl swiftly across the room to the kitchen, just as the door creaks open. Why didn't I stay home? *This is my home.* No! My home has been with Emil since the day I smelled his cologne mixed with the white roses. My neck and face are hot, and I'm fighting myself not to jump up and run.

"Schau. Ein Feuer, ich hab's dir doch gesagt." [*See. A fire, I told you.*] I hear scraping sounds at the fireplace.

"Ja, Bareis. Du hast wie immer recht." [*Yes, Bareis. You are right as always.*] Jäger's voice echoes off the walls. I clasp my hand over my mouth as tears pinch at my eyes. I squeeze my thighs tightly, holding back the urge to wet myself. *Emil, please come for me.* Suddenly loud crystalline crashes ring through the house from outside. Heavy footsteps rush through the front door. I peek around the corner of the kitchen counter to see Jäger still staring at the ashes, his head whips towards me just as I rear back around the counter. My eyes search frantically for anything within my reach that I could use to fight. I remember placing a loaded gun under the sink, for emergencies. I didn't want it in my room or my parents' room, so it seemed like the most natural place at the time.

I slow my breathing, open my ears and listen, hearing Jäger's footsteps slowly walking toward the kitchen, I poise myself to make it to the cabinet. I play out what will happen in my mind so I don't freeze once I begin, *reach the cabinet, open it, grab the gun, pull back the hammer, turn to him and shoot.* I lift myself to the crouching position, hoping I don't slip on my stocking feet, *1...2...*

"Jäger, komm', sieh her!" [*Jäger, come here!*] Jäger's footsteps turn quickly and head for the door, I complete a part of my plan, reaching the cabinet and grabbing the gun. I stick my head around again, ensuring my path is clear, then I run as quietly as I can down the hall to the back door of the cottage. I open the door just a hair and look out, confirming to myself that they are all still occupied out front. I push firmly to clear the landing, then leap through, run down the three small wooden stairs, searching wildly for where to go. The woods are only meters from the cottage, I start to run but hear slamming and crashing inside. I panic and freeze when the back door opens and sticks. They don't see me, the door is too large and it gets stuck on the broken rubber of the threshold I had intended to fix last summer. I look into the woods contemplating my options, *Run? Fight? Die?*, when I see a man in grey staring at me from the edge of the trees. He brings his fingers to his lips as to say "shh" then gestures his hand in a downward pressing motion. He has an exceptionally large gun hoisted up at this side. I do as he says. I crouch quietly to the ground, backing up as not to be seen as soon as they exit the door. I push to the edge of the cottage and don't feel any resistance where there should be against a wall. I look back and see a '*Victoire shaped*' hole that must have been created by a storm or flood since the last time I was here. I back into the hole all the way. I cringe as cold wet mud and gunk slide under my dress which pushes up to my waist because of the tight fit. A few multi legged bugs crawl over my arms and hands, I immediately start scratching at my hair, believing they have already made their way into my roots, leaving their eggs behind to hatch at a later date.

I continue to listen to the smashing and banging sounds above me inside the cottage, and I cry at the demise of my tiny pink and cream palace of solace. A pair of black shiny boots walk past my tiny hiding hole, then another and another. I hear their laughter and conversation. A cigarette falls to the ground, and the smell of German tobacco singes my nostrils...I sneeze, and the world stops. I see feet shuffling, searching for the source of the sound, then just as a grey knee hits the ground in front of my hiding place, his head follows suit, his eyes staring blankly into mine, with the entire side of his head blown open. Shot after shot rings out around me, inside the cottage, outside the cottage. I hold my gun tight in my hand instinctively cradling my head in my forearms as much as I can. Feet are running everywhere sounding like the pounding of elephants. Men are yelling in German and French...*Yiddish?* I see men retreating to the woods, the man in grey is running too, for a split second he looks behind him to my hiding place. I hear car engines whirring and tires digging and sliding over gravel, then the noises grow further and further distant. I stay where I am, staring at the soldier with half a face. I crawl slowly out of my hole, making it to all fours, then to my feet. Darkness descended long ago, I must have been staring at the soldier for ages.

I walk past him and make my way around the side of the cottage, my feet bare, and legs wobbling. I smooth out the front of my dress, collecting thick mud on the sides of my hands, bile ergs up my throat, but I swallow it back when I hear another car coming. This time I'm not afraid. To my advantage, there are no lights in the cottage. I look toward the car, and it looks familiar, but I can't be sure in this darkness, the moon isn't high enough to clear the trees and give me light. I sneak quietly through the front door and spot two figures about to open my bedroom door. I aim my gun, open my mouth, and force out my words.

"Arrêtez-vous! Mettez vos mains sur votre tête!" [*Stop! Put your hands on your head!*]

22

TOUCH

On a late afternoon
In a manor on the countryside
Two men go berserk

THE HOUSE OF HERR VON KONIG

Emil

I mmediately when we pull up to the house, I notice that the car is gone. My mind races with dreadful thoughts, *Did Jäger come back for her? Did she have to flee him? Had she decided to leave me after last night and go it on her own?* I could give a fuck about the car, but I can't lose Victoire. I'm opening my door before the car even stops, stumbling out and running into the house. Rolf and I both go mad looking for her. I scream her name throughout the house, checking her room for evidence that she has left me completely.

"Her bags are still here and her closet and drawers are still full of her clothes, so she hasn't left for good," Rolf assures me. I can't stop pulling my hands through my hair. I run outback and search for her, but I find nothing but an empty jam jar and a few breadcrumbs left behind by the little boy she doesn't think I know about. My eyes whip past the chicken coop and the empty garden bed that Victoire culti-vated over the summer with her own bare hands, which is now a mere square of cold dirt. I scream her name again.

"Victooooire!" A desperate emptiness takes over me. I need her. I turn back to the house meeting Rolf halfway in the corridor. "Rolf, I need to find her...I have to find her. God, do you think Jäger has been here, did he take her?" Rolf shakes his head slowly.

"No. But, I think I have an idea of where she is, let's go, it's getting dark." At his words, I race him to the car. I'm in the back seat ready to go as Rolf speaks with his man, then gets in next to me.

"Rolf, if she's left me, I just need to know she's safe," I fight the choking feeling in my throat.

"Emil, calm yourself, she hasn't left you, at least not yet," he chuckles, my head turns toward him slowly with all malin-tent in my eyes. "Hrrgh, hmm," he clears his throat, "Sorry." I tap twice on the partition and we leave the driveway. Within minutes I know we are heading to Victoire's cottage. I'm praying in my heart that she will be there. A little over a kilo-meter before the cottage, we see the car pulled to the side of the tree line, we stop and jump out shouting for Victoire. I scour the car and find nothing, while Rolf peers as best as he can through the trees. We hop back in the car and race to our destination.

The utopian little cottage with grey shutters is riddled with bullets. My knees go weak and almost give way, but my friend is there to hold me up.

"No. She's smart," he assures me, giving me just the slightest bit of hope, but when we walk through the door and flick my lighter, my heart sinks to my shoes, even Rolf's breath catches. Our eyes widen at the sight. Everything has been turned over, glasses and dishes broken, pictures of Victoire, her friends and family smashed. Moving to the bedrooms, we see beds slashed and the clothing that we left behind strewn across the floor. The blood in my ears is pounding, we only have one more room to search, *Please God let Victoire be alright, please*, just as my hand touches the doorknob, we hear a "click" behind us, coming from the front of the cottage.

"Arrêtez-vous! Mettez vos mains sur votre tête!" Rolf and I both do as she says, the hallway is dark and she cannot see us as the corridor is narrow with no windows, "Qui êtes-vous? Qu'est-ce que vous voulez?", [*Who are you? What do you want?*] her voice shakes. I can hear the metallic shaking of the gun in her hand.

"Victoire. C'est Emil et Rolf. Nous sommes ici pour vous ramener à la maison, mon Ange." [*Victoire. It's Emil and Rolf. We are here to bring you home, my Angel.*] At my words, I hear the gun drop and Victoire's footsteps running towards us. I open the last bedroom door letting in some moonlight allowing Victoire to see, she bypasses Rolf and jumps into my arms. I've never held anyone so tightly in my life, her soft hand caresses my cheek.

"Emil..." she whispers almost breathless, then faints in my arms.

Victoire

I WAKE up and I'm dizzy, not quite sure where I am. The last thing I remember is being at my cottage. I hit a rock that blew the tire, so I parked on the side of the road and walked to my little home. I shoot up and find I am lying in a bed in only a pair of pink silk taps. I hold the covers to my breasts and raise to my knees. I am in Herr von Konig's bed, in his blue room with the amber light. I look ahead to see Herr von Konig sitting at the hearth of his fireplace with his head down in his hands, still in his issue slacks, but only an A-shirt and bare feet outfit the rest of his body. He looks up at me with his face a cocktail of worry and anger. I brace myself.

"Did you leave me?" he asks, his timber low. I shake my head 'no' slowly, noticing the pins have been taken from my hair and it falls loosely to the tops of my shoulders, from the press I gave myself over the hot stove early this morning. I reach up and touch it, feeling my roots which have only gone back a little bit, then sliding my hand down to the edge of my tresses holding them loosely and sniffing in the faint scent of his cologne. I suddenly remember how frightened I was, how I flew into his arms early this evening, and he held me tight. "How do you feel," he stands, walking slowly toward me, stopping to lean on one of the posts of his bed.

"I'm fine," I whisper softly, enjoying the feel of his sheets against my bare skin, "A little sore." More memories flood to me. *Soldiers came to the cottage. I hid in a small crawl space. I scraped my knees. The ground was wet and cold.* I look down between myself and the sheet and see that I have been all cleaned up. I gasp looking up to Herr von Konig, with wide questioning eyes, he gives me his usual smirk. "D-did you b-bathe me?" His stare is intense as he nods his head 'yes'. I hold my hair again, "My hair?" his lips turn up just the slightest at the corners.

"...best I could do, I know how much care you take." I sniff the strands in my hand again.

"Thank you," I say with my head down. He nods, turning to leave the room.

"You put yourself in immense danger today," he growls angrily, turning his head slightly, giving me a profile view of his aquiline nose and strong chin, but he draws back his anger and speaks to me softly, "Rolf and I will go back tomorrow to see what we can salvage for you, until then, rest. I will see you in the morning."

"Herr von Konig," tears fill my eyes and my voice cracks. More memories assault my mind. *Emil, please come for me. My home is with Emil. White roses, cologne.* He stops at the door, his back tense with his hands in his pockets. "Emil," I cry out softly, tears burning me so I can't see. I wipe my eyes to see him staring at me, his hands still in his pockets but a strained look on his face, he steps toward the bed, gritting his teeth.

"Not, until you say Victoire." I double over in tears, the stress of the past few days, the past months hit me at once, and I need him. I don't want to beg, I want him to come to me, but he's right, it's what he said last night, and in his letter, that if I want his touch I'd have to give him permission.

"T-touche-moi, Emil."

He pulls his A-shirt roughly over his head, his strong muscular arms and abdominals flex with the motion, sending a chill straight through my body. He strides to the bed, "Je te sers mon Ange." [*I serve you my Angel.*] I watch with heated anticipation as he climbs onto the bed, I feel the mattress dip and sway under his weight, and with each movement he makes toward me I grow more and more nervous. I *want* to please him, I *want* to give him my body for his pleasure, I *want* to love him. He kneels before me, heaving quietly. His chest is a massive alabaster wall, pert cream color nipples rise and fall behind curly blonde hair that spans east to west, north to south as far south as I can see. I lick my lips at the thought of the delicious member that awaits me there. He raises his hands slowly, his palms facing toward me as if begging me not to run, *never*. His ocean blue eyes glaze over as he slowly lowers his lips to mine. He doesn't crush me; he gently asks me to open to him with a feather-light lick. I open, but it's not enough for him. He licks again, this time with his fingers holding my chin, and a quick succession of two wet laves; I obey his silent command. His lips are succulent and his kiss juicy and illicit. My eyes roll closed at the delicious feel of his tongue sliding languidly over mine. I cradle his face, deepening the kiss and ultimately forgetting that my hands were holding his bed sheet over my breasts. He reaches between us and yanks it down with a *snap*. My breasts are taut, and ready to feel the same patterns his tongue has been drawing inside my mouth. He ends our kiss, moving back slowly, a tiny glistening string of spittle follows his mouth from mine, when it breaks and falls to my chin, he wipes it away with his thumb, sweeping it across my nipple. I shudder feeling a hot flash of wetness form at my core.

His oceans wash over me again. "Mein Engel," he whispers while his strong, rough hands grab the backs of my thighs, firm but tender, pulling them apart in opposite directions, "Ich werde jetzt von dir naschen. Dein Honigkuchen reicht mir nicht länger aus," [*I will taste you now. Your honey cake will no longer sustain me,*] he slides two of his long brawny fingers inside me and I almost falter, but he holds me up, pulling me into his chest as he works a third finger inside, twisting around gently, stretching, searching for my--

"Ah!" my knee shoots up, landing my foot flat on the bed.

"Perfekt," Emil growls in my ear and in one swift movement, he releases me, lies on his back sliding his head between my thighs and takes a long searing lick up through the folds of my heat then back again. The action is overwhelming, I bend forward digging my hands into his waist, arching my back in extreme pleasure.

"Oh! Emil!" is all I can say as his mouth begins to consume me. His lips pull and suck at my petals while his tongue pulses in and out of my wet chamber. My hips instinctively rock back and forth over his mouth, spasmodic sequences that dip and glide, chasing the release he's promising me. I feel his hand grab my ankle, pulling my foot down and placing me back on both knees, he pushes me forward on my belly, and my arms splay forward. Emil finds my ankles again, flipping me over gruffly. I slip across the sheets as he drags me to him, higher and higher until only my head and shoulders are left touching on the bed, and my thighs are wrapped around his neck as he kneels above me. He wraps his forearm tight around my pelvis and his eyes close tranquilly as he takes me into his mouth again. I can't move my hips. I am powerless as he begins to suckle my clit, his beautiful pink lips and tongue slurping me in and out as his head gradually moves up and down, side to side. A white hot tightness swells in my womb, and I begin to shake uncontrollably. Emil brings his mouth over my entire mound, performing a wanton rouler une pelle [*roll and shovel*] with his tongue, and pulling from me the most intense pleasure I've ever known.

"Aah, Aah-heh, Aah, nnnaAAhhh, Aaaaaahhh!"

Emil

FUCK, Rolf was right. Victoire is pure treacle, and I would kill any and every man that tried to come between me and the taste that blooms on my tongue. As I make her cum a mélange of flavors delight me. "Hmmmmmpppff, Mmmwwwaaahmm, Hmmmm," I moan into her pussy in delicious triumph. Damp musk dances at my nostrils like the smell of the earth when I would go camping in the woods as a boy in Vienna. The nectarous essence of over ripe apricots, perfect for jam, slips over my taste buds, then yes, treacle, but the kind I lick is milky...molten. My eyes are hooded as I release Victoire, gliding her down my body gently. Once she is lying before me, my fingers reach for my belt buckle.

All I can hear is the sound of Victoire trying to catch her breath and the tiny clinks of my buckle coming apart. I push down my trousers and boxers, standing to the floor, and let them fall. I return to the bed and crawl to Victoire, watching her body make small impatient movements as she awaits me. I place my hands on her knees, kneeling between her legs. I glide them upwards massaging her thighs, my thumbs kneading her supple flesh, spreading her gently. I watch her as she hugs herself, bringing a finger to her mouth to suckle. I can't wait any longer to be inside of her. I softly tempt her core with two fingers, seeking out and flicking, that sensitive spot to make her melt.

"Hahhhhhaaaa...," she whimpers, quivering, lifting her hips to my touch, "Emil, please, uh, aauuhh." I insert a third finger twisting and thrusting, slowly widening her to welcome my girth. "Please," she whispers, imploring me for more. I honor her request, removing my fingers, licking off her nectar. I line myself up to her sheath and pray silently that I don't hurt her. The Österreich blood that courses through my veins has made me a man of generous proportions, not just in height. I bend down, and lay myself over her body, settling my full weight on my arms. I rest my forehead on the bed by her ear and caress her cheek, working my thumb into her mouth.

"Brace," I whisper. Victoire bites down, grabbing my wrist with both hands as I plunge into her warmth. My body shudders as she bathes my cock in her balmy wetness. I sink my teeth into Victoire's shoulder, muffling the groan that rattles in my chest.

"Aah," she coos again around the thick digit I placed in her mouth. I rock into her, long and slow watching as her lips part, her pretty blush tongue sliding around under the tender compression of my thumb. She bites a little harder with her pearly white teeth, and I hiss at the bit of pain that makes me grow even stiffer. I want to watch her satisfaction, so I raise her leg crossing it passed my chest, then over and down my waist, situating myself on her side giving me a full profile view of my Angel. She reaches her hands down, cupping them under my thigh, grinding her hips. The action squeezes her breasts together and I can't resist pulling a golden brown bud into my mouth.

Victoire

EMIL, Emil, Emil, is all I can think. The sensations he's pouring over me make me delirious. Every place on my body is taut and alert, waiting for his every touch, lick, kiss. He places his thumb in my mouth and I roll it around on my taste buds tart and sweet. I open my eyes just as he's about to enter me and I understand why he has made me this offering.

"Brace," he whispers in my ear, and before I can overcome my surprise at the thick, creamy length, he thrusts inside me. My eyes close at the pain which is soon soothed over with copious amounts of pleasure. He's so vast his staff tugs at my clit, when he enters me, dragging my juices over it.

"Aah," is all I sing as I'm bathed in ecstacy. I tremor over and over again, the fruits of multiple, mini-orgasmic sensations. Each time he pulls out from me, *tremor,* each time he advances, *tremor*. His ridged bellend drags along the sensitive internal flesh of my core, knocking me at my spot over and over. He pulls my leg up, crossing it over his broad chiseled chest, down passed the 'V' of his waist, to the top of his grand steel thigh, moving to my side. I reach down and cup my hands under it begging for more, grinding my slick pearl against his skin, the blond soir de mais hair on his legs providing lucious, tickling sensations. I arch my back as I feel his tongue flick at my nipple, then his mouth wraps around it so warm, switching between roughly and gently tugging. Emil pops his thumb from mouth and I roll my tongue around trying to find and recover the taste. Within seconds I feel him pinching my other bud, rolling it between his fingers, I cum without ceremony, giving him no cries of warning; it flows from me too fast.

The immediate aftershocks switch on my voice box, "Hhhaaaah, Emil!" My shouts fall on deaf ears as Emil continues ravishing my breasts, my only indication of his acknowledgment of my orgasm is his thrust growing faster, heavier riding straight through my cries for him. He grabs my ankle, stretching out my leg as he comes onto his knees. He rests it over his shoulder and his body becomes an engine. I listen to his deep panting breaths, feel his hand caressing up and down my leg. He brings my right leg around his waist, switching his stroke from fast and heavy, back to deep and long. His fingers move to dance over my clit, collecting nectar like a honey bee. He slows even more to a lazy heavy plunge, then a lingering withdrawal. He raises his fingers to his mouth, staring deeply into my eyes, *how is it possible he makes me nervous even now.* Slowly, and assuredly he takes a small lick, then offers them to me pressing gently against my lips.

"Taste us, mon Ange." I roll them around in my mouth tasting the heady mixture of brandy, and a musky sweetness that makes my eyes roll closed.

I pull my leg down from him and make my way up to my knees. With my hands, I urge him back against the bedpost. I grab the mahogany wood cylinder with both hands, trapping Emil between my breasts and the strong intricately carved post. Sliding down, kissing and licking his lips, I settle perfectly on top of his erection. We moan loudly in unison, my head reels back thrusting my breasts to his lips where he masters them, suckling and whirling...flicking and nipping. He grabs my hips and digs his fingers deep into my flesh, demanding control of his own pleasure, using my body to stroke himself. The very thought of myself being a tool for his own pleasure sends me over the edge, and I cum again, convulsing violently, kicking my legs outward and burrowing my nails into his shoulders.

"Fuck, Victoire," he growls, his eyes closed tight and a grimace of pleasure on his face. I pull away scurrying backward over the bed like a crab. He looks at me quizzically, his chest heaving, our breaths rapid, filling the room with the sound of breathlessness. His eyes flame and he lunges toward me, reaching out to grab me back...but it is my turn to taste.

Emil

WHY DID she pull away from me? I need her back. Heat lowers on my brow and a twinge of anger possess me for a moment's time. I reach out to grab her, and she moves back from me again up the bed toward the headboard, I follow reaching again, and again as she continually escapes my grasp. Frustration grips me until I submit. Moments later my head falls back on the pillows and I feel like all the wind has been knocked from my chest as Victoire lowers her warm mouth down over my rigid column. I try to raise my head to watch her, but each time I try a surge of pleasure races through my body, making me weak.

"Shit, Victoire," I hiss, taking in giant gulps of air while her tongue swirls around the head of my cock. Suddenly she pulls up and lowers her mouth down to my jewels, sucking them in, warming them, tickling them with her hums. My left hand shoots to my hair grabbing it at the roots while my right does the same to Victoire. We've been so passionate in our lovemaking my leg is dangling off the side of the bed while Victoire is on her hands and knees beside me, sucking me sideways. I finally gain enough strength to lift myself up on my elbow, as Victoire is moving gracefully up and down. I guide her, my hand still entwined in her hair. The warm glow of the fire light sets her pecan skin ablaze. I fall back again as another surge hits me, I shakily lift my leg back on to the bed, placing my foot flat down on the mattress into a mass of twisted, damp, sheets. I spread my legs, indulging in the pleasure of her head bobbing between my thighs. She licks the long vein under my shaft slowly, all the way up until she reaches my tip where she tickles me with her darting tongue. I feel the tingle of my release in my spine, moving like liquid fire to my cock.

"Uuh, Scheiße, Engel...Scheiße! [*Uuh, fuck, Angel...Fuck!*] Baby, I'm gonna cum!" My chest is hot and heaving, I try to pull Victoire away; I want the first time I cum to be inside her, but she refuses to let go. She relaxes her jaw imbibing me to the back of her throat, and my vision blurs as I cum intensely, jerking my hips with each powerful spurt. My Angel doesn't move away, she drinks from me, humming her approval. Her thirst finally quenched, she pulls back, bringing her fingers to her lips intently, swiping the remains of my cum into her sweet mouth, never taking her eyes from mine.

23

WHO IS HE, MAMAN?

On a settee
In a small sitting room
A daughter is in shock

CALIFORNIA | 1980

Lily

I fan my face with my hand, making a wolf whistle. "Whoa...okay Maman, chill," I say with my eyes wide. *Still fanning, by the way.*

"Chill? What is this chill," she scowls.

I chuckle and shake my head. "It literally means cool down", what you just told me was pretty steamy and I'm sure that was only half of it." Maman laughs at me, slapping her hands on her thighs.

"Oh, Chérie, all I said to you was that we finally kissed," my eyebrows shoot to the ceiling.

"No, Maman," I roll my neck and wag my pointer finger, "you said, you kissed WITH. YOUR. TONGUES. Then you were all up in his bed, where he made wild, passionate love to you until you were both dehydrated and the sun was coming up, then you said-"

"Sush!," she scolds me, looking away to the window with her lips knitted tightly. I rub my belly raising my eyebrows with a grin, waiting. Maman turns back to me with a bigger grin than my own. "It was a lovely time and I am not ashamed ma Chérie. We also made love in different ways." I nod my head understanding my mother. There are so many different ways to make love to a woman, not just physical. Our hearts are so much deeper than that. I think about my husband for a bit, how this morning he was up with the sun, checking the car, filling it with gas. Then he made me my breakfast of champions, toast with a smear of butter, boiled eggs and sauteed spinach. At the door before I left, he ran his hands through my hair massaging my scalp, kissed me like no tomorrow then watched me pull off...*that* is most definitely making love to a woman.

"From that night forward," Maman continues, pulling me from my thoughts of my husband, "we almost never left each other's side, except for when he had to work or obey his Father's requests in town. We went for long walks in the woods behind the house, we laughed *all* the time. I never knew how funny and mischievous he was before then. We went through his picture books and we talked about our families. He taught me German, in which, over time, I became proficient in short sentences," she chuckles. "He read poetry to me some nights in front of the fire, and I--," her cheeks darken with a crimson-esque glow, as she grins sheepishly, "and I performed for him other nights, a captive and very attentive and gracious audience," her smile grows wider, as does mine. "Ah, Chérie, there wasn't a single place in the house that was safe from us." I roll my eyes.

"Okay Maman!"

She chuckles wickedly, taking my hand and caressing it seductively. "Shall I tell you about the time he took me while I was baking bread in the kitchen," her eyes widen and she cackles.

"Eww, Maman!," I try pulling my hand away, screaming 'no', as she threatens to tell me more. She tickles my sides like she did when I was a child trying not to listen to her.

"Or shall I tell you about the time we had a snow drift and we ran out of wood so we had to *strruuuggle* to keep eachother warm!"

That's it.

"No!!," I scream, laughing wildly trying to cover my ears and my sides at the same time, "Maman, I have to pee!"

She rubs the sides of my belly like she's trying to warm me up.

"Okay mon Petite Ange, go!," she flicks her wrist, "And while you are there please have Lisette check on my honey cake and remind her of tea, I'd do it myself but..." she sighs picking up the photos again, her words trailing off. I return a few minutes later having relieved myself and discussing Maman's requests with Lisette, to discover my mother staring at a photo I haven't seen before.

"Who is that Maman, Lawd he's handsome," I say with my mouth agape. The sentiment is no understatement. The man in the photo is incredibly good looking. A cleft chin, dark hair and eyes that are so sorrowful they bore into my soul. A wide mouth is set perfectly under a trim mustache. I turn the photo over and see familiar handwriting on the back faded with time, and many swipes of fingers. I look from the picture to my mother whose face has greatly changed from when I left her laughing. My eyebrows furrow and my nostrils flare. I sit down slowly next to my mother and hold out the picture. I place my fingers under her chin and turn her face towards me, "Rolf?"

LETTERS FROM VATER

PART ONE

In a den
In front of the fire
A man is unfocused

THE HOUSE OF HERR VON KONIG | EARLY DECEMBER 1940

Victoire

"Aaah...Aaaahhh! Yes, yes, yes," I hiss as Emil pounds into me heavily from behind. He lifts his leg, his foot flush to the ground. He reaches a hand forward and grabs my shoulder, digging his fingers in hard to match the other set of fingers that are dug into my hip. His loud staccato pants, soon turn into deep, gruff grunts. I feel his sweat dripping onto my buttocks and the sensation forces me to cum for the fourth time since we've been making love, "Aaaah, Aaaaaah, Emil," I scream out between giant gulps of air, my body shaking with immense pleasure. Emil continues his focus. I look back to see him, his massive chest heaving, his abdominal muscles flexing, lifting and lowering, his arms rigid, holding me in place, his neck straining. His head is thrown back halfway giving me a view of his thick neck and that mesmerising Adam's apple that jumps as his licks his lips. The partial view of his face is twisted and furrowed, his teeth gnash tightly. He's holding back, trying to prolong his pleasure, which is unlike him. Emil enjoys taking his pleasure from me whenever and however, no need to prolong it, if it means we make love five times a day for his, and *my* satisfaction then sobeit, but never has he held on to his release.

"Autrichien. Cum," I command softly, and with those two words, Emil pulls out, strokes himself once and shoots white-hot laiche down my thighs. I'm beginning to resent when he does this, the more we grow with each other and make love, the more I dream of what a child with Emil would look like, *be* like. When we use the condoms he brings home from the pharmacy it doesn't bother me as much as it does when we've run out, which happens often, more than likely because I can't feel his essence dripping down my thighs as I can now. I clear my mind and bring it back to Emil, I'm still on all fours when I notice I have been in a daze for several minutes. I feel Emil behind me with a warm cloth, wiping me down gently. I stretch like a cat, then lie down on my stomach. We relax in silence, but I know something is wrong.

"Emil?"

"Hm," his grunt of acknowledgment is deep and distant.

"What's wrong? Don't say 'nothing' I know you well, something is troubling you, you're angry." Emil inhales and holds his breath, I rise up on my elbow and lay my head on my hand, waiting. He exhales, raising himself from his lying position, raising his knees to his chest and resting his arms there. I continue to wait; I hate to push him.

"Vater sent me another letter." I sit up and caress my hand down his back feeling his tensed muscles relax for a moment at my touch.

"What does he want?"

Emil's jaw ticks at my question. His neck and face turn red, and he looks at me with intense eyes and his smirk.

"Ha!," he laughs incredulously, "He wants to visit!"

I reign in the sudden fear I feel. From everything Emil has told me about his Father, this request to visit can't be good, but I want to calm him not irritate him more by expressing my reticence. I scoot closer, pressing my breasts into his side and laying my head on his shoulder.

"Maybe he just wants to come and see you, make sure you are well," I say smoothly and calmly, still caressing his back. He looks down at me again, then presses his lips hard against my forehead, kissing several times. We sit quietly for a long time, entwined in each other's limbs, just thinking, contemplating, listening to each other breathe while memorizing the feel of our shoulders, knees, nail beds. Finally, Emil breaks the silence.

"I believe he is coming because of Jäger." My neck snaps back and my brow furrows.

"Jäger? Why?"

He shakes his head, tapping the floor with his finger, huffing. "The same reason why *most* wealthy families are always in each other's business," he sighs heavily, "our father's know each other, and they gossip" he says matter of factly, "In fact, I believe that is the very reason why he hasn't made some desperate attempt at coming back here to settle our 'disagreement'." My body tenses, remembering what Jäger said to me that night in the kitchen, then I remember he was at my cottage, he must have known it was mine, there were pictures of me and my family everywhere, I turn to Emil.

"There is something I didn't tell you," he looks at me, examining the worry swept across my face.

"Qu'est-ce que c'est mon Ange? Dites-moi," [*What is it my Angel? Tell me,*] he replies softly. His ocean blue eyes are drowning me, holding me under, I have to look down so I can come up for air.

"It's about Jäger." Emil licks his bottom lip and bites down hard, as if trying not to curse, his hands hold mine a little tighter. "That night in the kitchen," I begin, but he stops me.

"No," he shakes his head, turning to look at anything else but me, "That is done, it's finished, and frankly Victoire," he says standing to his feet, his voice deepening, "I don't want to ever hear you utter his name again." I pull the small blanket we brought to the floor up over my body and stand up to meet his gaze, but he is indignant, hands on hips, breathing deep, and his hard jaw set tightly...still shaking his head. I move closer, placing my hands on his bare chest.

"Please Emil, you must listen, please," he calms down and gives me his full attention, "if you believe your father's visit is connected to Jäger, then maybe we should leave," he looks at me questioningly, "that night in the kitchen with *him*, I did not want his advances, you must know this," more indignance, "Stop. Listen," I plea, "you must *know* this. I know it looked differently, poorly, but it wasn't what you thought. Jäger came into the kitchen saying he was looking for the bath, but then he wouldn't leave. He started telling me how beautiful I was, 'for a schwarze'…" at those words Emil practically jumps at me, his ire coiling his body to fight. "Emil," I call to him, I know his mind is distant.

I caress his cheek and place a hand over his heart, I feel it racing, heat flowing off his body like a furnace. I decide not to finish telling him the rest because it doesn't matter, not if it makes him so vehemently angry. Ruining the time we spend together is never worth it, "Emil...it's okay, shhh," I pat his chest and lift my head, standing on the tips of my toes to kiss his chin, "nevermind, my love, it's alright. Let's listen to some music, okay? I will sing for you." I move toward the record player, but Emil catches my wrist, and pulls me tightly into his arms, I can't move. He bends his head down next to my ear and inhales deep through his nose.

"What. Else. Did. He. Say." he whispers through gritted teeth. I tap my forehead to his chest and continue.

"He said that he was always curious about black women and since my mother was Quadroon maybe the Fürher would forgive his curiosity," Emil's arms wrap tighter as his breathing becomes less easy, "I told him to leave, and that is when he said that if I didn't allow him to have his way, he would report you for–for," my voice lowers, "métissage," [*miscegenation*] Emil's grip loosens until I am almost out of his arms. "I couldn't bear the thought of losing you, of sending you to some God awful prison because of me...because of something that I could control...a simple act to ensure your safety," tears well in my eyes and my throat tightens, "so I let him push me onto the table and..." My voice trails off, I'm so ashamed I can't look at him, when I finally build the courage to allow my eyes to glance at his, the shame is doubled when I see the pained look on his face.

He takes a step back, then another...another, alternating between shaking his head and looking up to the vaulted ceiling, masking slowly flowing tears of frustration, "Why didn't you tell me," he chokes out.

"Your temper. I didn't want you to do something that would land you in jail anyway, I thought if I let it happen, if I kept quiet everything would be fine. You and Rolf interrupted before it went too far."

"Fine!? Too far!?" he shouts. I swear cracks form in the walls from the boom of his voice, and I jump.

Emil

ABSOLUTELY NOTHING about this situation was fine, nothing. This prick had insulted her, held her emotionally hostage with a threat to my freedom, then taken advantage, nearly abusing her body. No, there was nothing fine. On top of this, I thought she wanted him. She looked willing and I'd almost killed her for it. If she had only told me, that night never would have happened. We wouldn't have gone through that hell, but the more I think about it while I look at her now, standing in front of me trembling in the face of my anger, I know that we would have been in a different hell, me jailed for killing Jäger, and Victoire sent away to God only knows where. My only solace would have been the hope that Rolf would have absconded somewhere with her to keep her safe. I count backward from ten in my head to extinguish the flames roving about my body, my anger is not with Victoire, it should never have been, it is with Jäger. I regain the two steps I took back from her and reach out to touch her beautiful face.

"Mein Engel," I begin, "Ich würde eine Million Gefängnisstrafen in Kauf nehmen, nur um bei dir zu sein," she shakes her head not knowing what I've just told her, I drop down to my knees, wrap my arms around her thighs and rest my head on her soft womanly belly. I look up and pour my soul into her brown almond-shaped eyes as I repeat each word for her understanding, "My Angel. I would go to jail a million times, just to be with you." Her lips engage mine the moment I say it. We tangle ourselves in each other, caressing and wiping away tears, offering heart-wrenching apologies between soft, wet, passionate kisses. We dissolve into one another for hours.

As she sleeps in my arms I think about her words, '*If you believe your father's visit is connected to Jäger, then maybe we should leave*', but where too? Try as I might, the only place I can think of to keep Victoire safe is here, in my home in the countryside. Hitler wouldn't dare destroy Paris, his precious treasures are here, but what if he wins, then where will I and Victoire be? He won't win, he can't, this shitstorm won't last forever. I just need to keep her safe until then, but I won't run from Jäger and I definitely won't run from my Father, I have nothing to hide. My heart lurches at that sentiment, the truth is, I do have something to hide, something more precious than all the diamonds and rubies in the world, and she is sleeping right here, in the crook of my arm.

25

INTEL

The Bliss Family Residence
In the large hollow den of Herr Heinrich Bliss
A phone conversation commences

VIENNA | EARLY DECEMBER 1940

Heinrich Bliss

Bliss: "So, my son is still at these games?"

    Intel: "Jawohl, it seems so Herr Bliss. This looks poorly on your family, you understand. The tide has shifted immensely, yet you have not reigned in your son. As one of Vienna's wealthiest families, it would be in your best interest to resolve this matter, ja?"

I lower my head to my hand on my wide oak desk and breathe deeply.

Bliss: "Of course, I will make my plans."

Intel: "We suggest you do this quickly."

Bliss: "And why is that?"

Intel: "There is a baby…and an impending marriage."

Fire rages through me.

Intel: "You know the laws…*buuut* apparently your son does not. Your money and privilege help to shield you…but not for long. Make your plans, do it quickly."

I hang up the phone and do as the voice says.

ES IST EIN ROS ENTSPRUNGEN

Two nights before Christmas
In a nice warm bed
In a blue room with amber light

THE HOME OF HERR VON KONIG | DECEMBER 1940

Emil

I t's almost Christmas. Victoire and I should both be home with our families and friends wrapped warmly in smiles and hugs from those we love. Instead, we are here in the throat of war, living just outside of the lion's den. Our only relish is the time we spend together wrapped in each other's arms. We've made love all evening long, and now we lay here quietly, watching the fire dance. The low buzz of jazz plays from the record player in the corner of my room.

I feel Victoire's hand move slowly across my neck. She

nuzzles against me, placing slow, warm, lazy kisses on my chest.

"Yes, mon Ange," I whisper into the glowing darkness, smiling, keeping my eyes on the fire. The feel of her lips on my skin is akin to the heat of the orange flames.

"I have a present for you." She smiles shyly into my arm, hiding from me. I rise to my elbow in surprise.

"What is it? Come on," I giggle "What is my present?" I commence to giving her light tickles on the sides of her breasts and tummy until she finally decides to give.

Biting the tip of her thumb, Victoire is soon out of my reach, and across the room lifting the needle off the record. I watch as her high, ample cheeks wiggle away from me, sending a rush of blood to my member. I will never get enough of her.

She bends down and pulls out a small square package wrapped in brown paper. I shake my head smiling, wondering what she's about to show me until she removes a black record from the brown paper.

"I-I paid a girl from the neighboring village to buy it," she tells me nervously.

"Liebeschen!" I growl, making my way to her in two strides, "You know that is dangerous! Why do you insist on placing yourself in precarious situations!?" My heart breaks as she looks down at the floor. Once again, my temper precedes me, scolding her like a child. I only want to keep her safe. We already play too close to the edge living alone together and becoming lovers. With SS searching for Resistance throughout the countryside, Jäger's attempt on her very person and the letter from Vater, I have increased my vigilance at keeping her secure. I would surely die for her. I will never lose her, especially for something as small as a Christmas gift, for me.

I would also die before I broke her spirit. "Forgive me, my love. Please forgive me, I only think of you. I am sorry, forgive me." I bow myself over her lap and her body quivers slightly. "Please my love. Do not be afraid, forgive me...forgive me," I whisper reverently kissing her fingers.

Victoire

I KNOW he only means to protect me. I forgive him the moment he asks it of me. I lean down and kiss the back of his head. His blonde hair is radiant in the firelight and smells of fresh bergamot. I place the needle on the record.

"Your present," I whisper softly in his ear. I go back to caressing his cornsilk strands, letting the music carry me as I sing to him, shakily at first, but growing in strength once he recognizes the melody.

> *"Es ist ein Ros entsprungen*
> *Aus einer Wurzel zart*
> *Aus uns die Alten sungen*
> *von Jesse kam die Art*
> *Und hat ein Blümlein bracht*
> *Mitten im kalten Winter*
> *Wohl zu der halben Nacht..."*

Tears stream from his ocean blue eyes. Before I can complete the song, he reaches out with his strong arms and pulls me to him.

Emil

I HEAR nothing but her glorious, silvery voice floating to my ears. The music cannot compete, it simply ceases to exist. I embrace her so tightly I feel I might break her. I'm over-whelmed and for a moment have forgotten to be gentle.

"Mon Ange. Wh-when...h-how did you learn?" My eyes sting as fond memories of Christmases as a boy come back to me. My mother would take me to visit her family, leaving Vater behind. It would be wonderful days and nights filled with exuberant cousins, gift shopping at the markets, and filling our bellies with delicious Sachertorts, and kinderpunch for us children. I can hardly contain my joy and sadness. I hug her, kissing her face all over, from her cheeks to her nose and forehead, then her lips.

"I learned while you worked. Sometimes late at night while you slept, without the music, just the words and the notes. I found a book in the attic of Christmas music and there it lay before me. I remembered you telling me you loved this song as a small boy, how your mother used to sing it to you at night to calm you to sleep so that Père Noël would finally come."

I let out a childlike giggle and repeat her words while caressing her cheek gently with the backs of my fingertips.

"Père Noël."

"Oui mon amour, Père Noël."

I pull her lips to mine, softly whispering Père Noël, over and over, brushing the tip of my nose against hers. My Angel has given me a gift...a gift that no one can ever pilfer. I will take her song and lock it away in my heart forever. No matter where I go, or if we should ever be apart. I can unfold her psalm from my heart like a secret letter...her voice an indelible ink etched across the plain.

Victoire

"MON AMOUR." I reach up, swiping my fingers along his cheek. I bring them to my tongue tasting the salty liquid that flows from the bluest oceans, here in the bluest room. He licks his lips and takes my mouth, pulsing out his tongue, begging me to open to him. I do, willingly and we tangle together softly for long moments. My hands then fly to the nape of his neck and skip down his chest as he begins placing hot, wet kisses along my jaw, then my neck and décolletage.

Emil licks and nips at my delicate flesh. His salivation increases my pleasure as his moist aperture captures my stiffened peaks. His tongue plays at me as he looks up, tapping the very tip to each bud, then flicking them gently. His eyes lower, as if torn between watching me or watching my buds expand under the tutelage of his tongue. I don't care which he chooses, so long as he doesn't stop.

He lays us down continuing to flick and suckle. My whimpers of pleasure fill the room, as my body yearns for more. Emil pays attention and moves his hand slowly down my belly tickling me playfully.

Emil

I CIRCLE my thumb around her belly button, watching the fire light flicker over her beautiful smile. I walk my fingers down past her dark curly hair and began to play at her clit, soft and wet, pressing it tenderly with my fingers making slow tender circles, coaxing out her precious nectar. Victoire breathes in deeply. She brings her knees together to savor my touch then languidly opens her legs wide for me.

The circling and flicking of my fingers make her rock up

and down in search of more. She places her hand on top of mine encouraging me to give her what she needs. I release the plump, rich nipple in my mouth and raise to my knees, her plush pecan body melts under my touch. Her dark brown tresses shine in the fire light. I watch as she brings her hand to her mouth and begins sinfully sucking on her finger. Her ruby red lips form the most delectable 'o' as she slowly opens her eyes. Her gaze rushes all my blood swiftly through the length of my manhood.

"Autrichien. Prenez-moi." [*Austrian. Take me.*] I yank her legs to me, wrapping them around my waist. With one long, smooth, thrust I am inside her. Inside the most lush, warm and bountiful garden where one day I intend to plant seeds. One day when this war is behind us.

A groan eases from my chest as I rock, once, deeply inside my Victoire. My schwanz jumps at the sounds of her pleasure, faint purrs that rattle softly in her throat. I groan again as her fingers sink into my forearms, sending delectable shocks of painful pleasure through my body. I sustain my vocal appreciation, stilling myself, waiting patiently for her to adjust to me. Our hands intertwine and I bring them to my chest, bending over her perfect frame. I plunge into her again and again; flares of pleasure race through my groin down to my toes.

I feel her wetness slick between us. I reach down between her velvet cheeks and sop up her dew with my finger. I don't miss a single stroke while I feed myself, delighting in her essence on my tongue.

Victoire

THE SIGHT of Emil licking me from his fingers increases my arousal.

He bends to my ear, "Mmmmm, Aprikosen," he moans. I smile. The vibrations of his voice mixed with his panting breaths sensually tickle my neck.

"Ah," I sigh, meeting his cadence. His deep guttural utterances wave over my skin. He has taken to teaching me new, delicious words while we make love and I am his willing student. He dips his fingers again then slows his pace to take a long obscene lick of his digits. His pink, glistening tongue finds its way into my mouth where he lingers. He breaks our kiss watching me, biting his lip, waiting for me to repeat. His pace is intense and slow.

"Say it."

"A-pri-ko-sen." I mimic lazily, searching his eyes for meaning.

"Apricots," he whispers, twirling my hair. My breath hitches at my understanding of his term for my taste on his lips. He nuzzles the crook of my neck, thrusting powerfully. "Mein Aprikosenbaum … *aahhhh* mein Engel … immer reif, in voller Blüte … *ähm* … dein Nektar ist so süß ... und nur für mich. Du bist mein Schatz, meine Liebe, ich werde dich niemals gehen lassen." [*My apricot tree ... aahhhh my Angel ... always ripe, always blooming ... uuh.... your nectar is so sweet ... just for me. You are my Precious, my Love, I will never let you go.*]

He raises to his knees again, bringing me with him. My legs are still wrapped around his waist and I grind slowly burying him deeper with every motion. My eyes roll back with the mounting pleasure between us–higher and higher.

Emil

I GRAB her waist and watch as she grinds and spears herself on me repeatedly.

"Emil!"

Her walls clench around my cock announcing her burgeoning orgasm.

Cords of gruff, unintelligible groans release themselves from my throat, spurred on by the stirring sensation in my jewels.

I want to plant my seed inside her. Give her my warmth, marvel at the glistening moisture of our shared love when I pull out of her. The thought of Victoire swollen with our child pushes me over the edge and I'm ready to cum hard, but now is not the time for new life. Each time we make love it gets harder and harder to pull away from her. Sweat forms on her brow, as she works hard for her pleasure. My long, thick schwanz massages the soft inner flesh of her pussy with every advance.

"Mon Ange, let go." She doesn't obey me, she locks her legs tighter. "Victoire," I growl low in warning of my release.

"Non, I want to feel you." Just at that moment, her orgasm hits. Her legs tremble and she grits her teeth against the hard pulses of delight that flow through her. I struggle against my own climax.

Victoire

I GROW weary of him pulling away and cumming anywhere but inside me; I want all of him. I wrap him in a death grip to force his hand, but he has twenty times my strength.

"Victoire, I can't hold on anymore! Stop. Stop it! Lass los!" [*Let go!*] His hands are like vices as they drag me from his body. With one harsh move, he yanks me up and off his cock and lands me gently on my belly. He cums with staggered grunts and gulps, stroking himself as his white hot cum shoots over my thighs and buttocks.

"Aaah, Scheiße, uh! Nghhaa Scheiße. Victoire."

Emil

I HATE myself in these moments, it's not what I want. Victoire's whimpers and sniffs stab me in the chest. I pinch the bridge of my nose tamping down the sting behind my eyes.

"Fuck!"

I stomp to the bathroom to fetch a warm cloth to clean her. I turn on the light and look at myself in the mirror. I splash cold water on my face and there, a familiar pair of blue eyes stare back at me jealously, for having what this Nazi bastard in the mirror doesn't deserve. Safety, security and a woman–a goddess, to love him, serve him...deliver him. I yank a white, pristinely folded towel from the ring, run it under hot water then make my way back to my Angel. Kneeling down I bathe her gently, marveling at the smooth, beautiful pecan hue of her skin.

Victoire keeps her face turned away from me. She's begun to hate me when this happens, the pleasure is short lived, she desires more. I, myself have wondered about a bonnie, little, tawny skinned babe with blue eyes and tight curly brown hair? He would have Victoire's smile and laugh and my determination. I'd be damned if I would hide my child, or pretend the seed in her belly belonged to some farm hand in the next village, *No.* They would surely imprison us...kill us? With Jäger sniffing around and Vater up to God knows what, Victoire would have to understand.

"Mon Ange," I whisper to her, invading her sadness "one day, I promise...one day we will be free from this place. We will have children—and we will love them and feed them your honey cakes until they are fat." We both giggle sadly at my attempt at humor. "Und we will watch them grow. One day the seeds from our garden will smile up to us, with shining faces, Versprochen. [*I promise.*] I love you...with everything that I am, mein Engel...I promise."

LETTERS FROM VATER

PART TWO

Two nights before Christmas
In an opulent yet desolate apartment in
  the city
A man receives a box

THE PARIS APARTMENT OF HERR ROLF BLISS |
DECEMBER 1940

Rolf

I stumble into my apartment, drunk as usual. It's the only thing nowadays that keeps me from the sadness I feel not being with Ayouba and our son. I pull the picture from my breast pocket and look at it longingly. My beautiful Ayouba holds our newborn son next to her cheek, proudly smiling into the camera. My eyes well with tears and I slam my back against the door, searching to find a physical pain to mask the pain in my heart. She sent a note along with the picture saying how much she missed me and that my family was waiting for my return. Since then I've heard nothing. I have written letter after letter. I cannot go to her. I will *not* endanger them. Not Ayouba, her parents and brothers, or our 6-month-old child, little Rolf. I die another death every day I wake up without them. The only things besides this bottle that keep me sane are Emil and Victoire. Victoire reminds me of Ayouba, so smart and brave, beautiful. Speaking to Victoire helps me feel like I'm speaking to Ayouba.

I slide down to the floor and my thigh crunches on a box. "Shit!" I hiss out as the edge sticks into me. My mind wonders how the hell this box arrived in my home. *Doesn't really matter, it's here.* I push myself up off the floor, pick up the box then head to my bedroom where I place it on my desk. I sniff around the room, scrunching my nose at the stench. Looking around and seeing everything in its place, I sniff my underarms and find that the stench is indeed me.

"You'll have to wait," I point at the box, noticeably slurring my words. I'm so shit-faced right now. I take off my clothes then head to the bathroom where I take my fourth piss of the hour then run the bathwater hot. Once full, I sit in the tub and let my mind drift to Ayouba and my little Rolf. I smile as I watch them play by the ocean, I can almost hear their squeals and giggles as I see myself running towards them. I make my way to Ayouba's side as she spins with little Rolf smiling toothlessly in her arms. I reach out to take them in my embrace and begin to cough and choke. I open my eyes and struggle to catch my breath. I must have fallen asleep and slipped under the water. I scrub myself and empty the tub. Dressing in my robe I thank God I have my man start a fire in my room every night. Though the embers are burning low, it's still warm. I throw on another log then head to my bed. From the corner of my eye, I see the box, I had forgotten all about it. I toil with waiting 'til morning to open it, but curiosity gets the better of me and I take a seat at my desk. Unwrapping the brown paper, I uncover a black square box tied with white string stamped with my family seal. I roll my eyes.

"What fresh hell is this," I sigh. More than likely another one of Mother's extravagant party invitations, like the year she sent out over one hundred custom-made snow globes that had the invitation to her annual New Year's Eve party engraved on the bottom. It was a disaster. Half of them ended up broken on arrival and the other half, no one bothered to turn the globe over to see the invitation. A week out from the party she had only received two RSVPs, frantic she hired a service to go to each invitee's home and deliver the message verbally. My father was embarrassed and livid with her the entire year.

I chuckle, wondering what the surprise will be this year. I pull the string cracking off the seal and open the box. Immediately, my blood turns to ice. Before me is every letter I had written to Ayouba since she sent me the picture. My eyes widen with dread and my heart cracks open inch by inch, each second. My hands fly to the letters, flipping through each one touching them, counting them, each one in pristine condition save for a long single slit at the top. My eyes are wide darting from letter to letter, a stabbing pain cuts through my chest mimicking my heartbeat, rapidly stabbing. When I get to the bottom of the box, my fingers tremble. One last letter in a cream envelope remains.

My father's handwriting.

I pick it up almost dropping it, everything has become weak. I open it and begin to read slowly.

My Son,

 Since the day you were born you have been the pride

and joy of my life. I know you may not believe so, but it is true. Everything I have ever done in life has been to assure you and your mutter would be safe and well taken care of, everything. From the moment I took you from your mutter's breast and held you I knew that every breath I took from that moment on would be to give you the absolute best, and with that best is the Bliss family name. Though our name is not without blemish, it is nothing that we cannot--could not overcome in time with hard work. However, there is something from which our name would never recover, and that is the shame your actions would have brought upon this family should I have allowed you to carry on as you have the last two years. I have allowed your frivolous dalliances, your trips across the world to parts unknown to pick up useless shards of pottery and paintings, your parties and even the home you secretly purchased with money from your trust. But to carry on as you have cavorting with some heathen African woman, impregnating her and promising to give her your family's last name in marriage, that is far enough. Your mutter and I have chosen well for you in Dorothy Schneagle, why do you think we sent her and her sister to you in Marrakech? She is to be your bride. The embarrassment we have endured from her family by her reports on how you treated her so rudely has been almost insurmountable, your mutter was beside herself. Not to worry, I have not told her about your black harlot or bastard child, it would kill her, and I would not bring such misery on her head.

I love you my son, and one day you will understand why I did this, it was all for you, for our family. You will recover quickly, as you are strong, you are a Bliss. Think of this woman no more. To help you succeed in your progress, I

*have removed her and her family as an issue. They exist no
more as of the time you receive this letter.*

*Your mutter and I expect to see you at her New Year's
Eve party, we will talk further then, my son.*

Your vater,

Heinrich Bliss

My entire body shakes uncontrollably. I turn the envelope upside down, and a tiny 'clank' sounds out into my room like a canon. My fingers jitter as they move slowly to the white tissue that housed the metallic sound. I peel away the rumpled folds and creases, and there before me is my signet ring. I hadn't noticed the red stains on the tissue it was wrapped in until I saw the color smeared across the 'B'. My body jerks forward and I vomit all over myself. I heave and heave. An unfamiliar voice purges itself from my throat, from the depths of my soul, a demon wailing. Once it escapes, I have no voice left. Unable to breathe a second longer, I reach into my desk drawer. Pull out the Luger. Open my mouth, and pull…

The beach.

My beautiful Ayouba and my little Rolf smile at me, warm in my arms.

~

EARLY THE NEXT Morning

It is cold

THE HOME OF HERR VON KONIG

Emil

A distant thumping opens my ears, I frown, then turn over. I'm cold. I reach for my Victoire and pull her close. She's warm and soft, immediately stiffening my cock. I burrow myself between the plump cheeks of her bottom and kiss her shoulders and neck. My Angel stretches, arching her back pushing her ass further back on my shaft gently wiggling back and forth. With her eyes still closed, half asleep, she rolls to her back.

"Autrichien," she yawns with a great sigh, I love how she has taken to simply calling me 'Austrian', it tickles me, "it's so early." I bend my head down and take a turgid nipple in my mouth and suckle from her as if she is feeding me. With a moan she stretches wide, spreading her legs. My fingers dive anxiously down to her kitzler where they softly rub and tug to her delight. She arches again, and again as the pleasure I give her rolls over her body.

"Emil," she whispers, breathless.

Bang! Bang! Bang!

We both shoot up, looking at each other, startled. No one comes to visit us out here except for Rolf, and it's way too fucking early for him to make an appearance. Confused, I give Victoire a short peck on the lips.

"Wait, here," I command. I move to the small chairs in front of my bed and pick up my robe.

Bang! Bang! Bang!

I look at Victoire to assure her everything is alright, as she sits up on her knees with the covers wrapped tightly around her body.

Bang! Bang! Bang! Bang!

I tear out of the room, "Okay! Ich komme! Scheiße!" [*Okay! I'm coming! Shit!*] I make it down the stairs to the vestibule, then the front door, opening it wildly, ready to pounce, when I see Rolf's man, his driver, standing at the front door about to pound on it again. He reaches back, the hat in his hand is damn near crumpled.

"S'il vous plaît, docteur von Konig, vous devez venir avec moi immédiatement. C'est Herr Bliss! [*Please Dr. von Konig, you must come with me immediately, it's Herr Bliss!*] His red eyes dart from me to the ground, then back. I invite him in, but he refuses, restating his request firmly, "Non monsieur, maintenant! Vous devez venir!" [*No, Sir now! You must come!*] My mind races. Rolf must be drunk or hurt. I implore his man to wait where it is warm so I can get dressed, he nods and takes a weary seat on the bench. Back inside I see Victoire, wide-eyed at the top of the staircase.

"I told you to stay in the room Angel," I say softly, caressing her cheek once I reach her. I lead her back to bed, then head to the closet and dress quickly.

"What's wrong," she questions with worry in her voice. I shake my head as I yank up my boots and grab my black doctor's bag.

"I don't know, Rolf's man is downstairs, shaken. He says I must go with him. I shouldn't be long, perhaps an hour, will you make some strong coffee and bacon. Rolf will need something on his belly. I'm going to bring him here, more than likely he's binged again.

Victoire nods 'yes' and heads to her room to dress. I turn and watch her in irritation. I look toward the vestibule but decide to follow her to her room instead.

"Victoire," she turns to me, her brow pinched in concern.
"Yes?"

"Today we move all of your things over to our room." I nod my head once, commanding her understanding of my statement. She gives me her infamous coy smile, biting her bottom lip then heads toward her bathroom. I slap my hand on her door in triumph, then make for the stairs, not knowing that in 30 minutes, my whole life would be turned upside down.

∾

5 hours later

THE HOME OF HERR VON KONIG

Emil

A FRANTIC VICTOIRE meets me at the door. I hear nothing. When my eyes finally focus on her, I look around and I don't even know how I got here. I look down and see the black box gripped in my hands. I fall to my knees and weep. My friend, my confidant, my brother is gone. I feel Victoire's hands moving about my body, there is blood and grey matter from my neck to my waist. When I saw him I tried to pull him up, to wake him. Delirium. I had lost all medical knowledge. I pulled, screaming, pleading. There is blood on my back and down my pants from when I slipped in his blood, nonsensically trying to drag him to his bed. The air was thick and putrid from the stench of the dried vomit and ruin...*he'd urinated himself.*

"He's g-g-gon-nah," is all I can get out between gasps for air. Victoire holds me tight rocking me, allowing me to burden her with my sorrow.

She holds back her own tears, trying to provide a strength I need, *my woman.*

∾

2 weeks later

THE HOME OF HERR VON KONIG

Emil

I PLACE a picture of Rolf in the corner of my dressing mirror and slip his signet ring on my pinky finger. I told his father I had no idea where it had gone and those are the last words I will ever utter to that man or his wife again. Victoire slips quietly behind me, wrapping her arms around my middle, letting her hands slide up to my chest. She provides a warmth and comfort I've never known and will cherish forever. I hate that she couldn't come to his funeral.

"Where will they take him," she asks, her cheek pressed against my back.

"Back to Vienna."

She breathes in sharply, screeching and pushing away from me.

"They're going to keep him separate from them? Even in death!? He belongs with them in Marrakech! Why didn't you say something, Emil!? Why didn't you say something!?"

I pull her to me and hold her tight, taking my turn to offer comfort. She tries to pull away, but I hold tighter until she stops, until she is reduced to a soft cloud, showering my chest with tears. The truth is there would be nothing left in Marrakech, nothing more than a hope? I am certain of what his father did, and more than likely there is no burial sight for them. I pray silently that they are all together now in heaven.

The next few weeks whirl by. An unceasing string of days that run one into another. A loud, deafening silence blankets the world like fallen snow, my friend...my brother, is gone.

2 8

RUN!

A few hours before dawn
To a sleeping house
Visitors descend

THE HOME OF HERR VON KONIG | LATE
FEBRUARY 1941

Emil

Victoire's back is turned to me as she makes her way through the woods out back. We've just finished making love. I taste her on my lips, I can feel the sweat dripping down my back, it's cold and makes me shiver. I blink and see her walking faster. She's naked and shivering. I run into the house to grab her robe to take to her, and just as I turn around Rolf is there, his eyes sunken and dark. I smile, happy to see him but he doesn't return the greeting. Instead, his face twists into a harsh grimace and he begins to shout.

Though I'm only inches away I can't make out what he's saying.

"I can't hear you, Rolf!" He's still shouting, pointing toward Victoire. I look back and she is still in the woods, still walking swiftly, still shivering. A strong force turns me back to Rolf. I reach for him to shake him, but my hand doesn't meet his flesh. He shouts silently, straining, pointing, sunken eyes now bulging. "I can't hear yoooouuuuu!" I shout angrily. Another force pushes me toward him. I'm just about to reach his arm when I finally hear him…

"RUN!"

I shoot up from bed, sweating and panting heavily. It's been weeks since I collected Rolf's things from his apartment, more weeks still since his death. The dreams are getting more and more vivid, but this was the first time I've been able to hear what he's been trying to say to me these past several days. Always the silent shouting. Always Victoire in the woods. But each time the force pushes me toward him, I wake up. I let my eyes adjust to the darkness, then look to my left to see Victoire, warm, curled in a ball in one of her pretty silk nightgowns. I reach over to touch her, but think better of it, my hands are cold and clammy. I squint my eyes and look at the clock above the fireplace, *5 am. Sheesh.* I have to be up in an hour, I have patients all day. I reach back for my pillow, noticing the familiar dampness from the exertion of my dream, I do my best to fluff it to help me fall back to sleep. Just as my head hits the soft goose down, I hear the whirring of engines. I leap up from the bed to look out the window. Outside in the darkness, I make out two utility vehicles and one long car. Heat races through my chest and I make my way to Victoire.

"Victoire," I shake her, no time to waste. "Victoire, you must wake up, now!" She rubs her eyes and yawns.

"Autrichien, it is early, but I will have your breakfast," she starts stretching her arms. I gruffly shake her again, desperately needing her to pay attention to me. I grab her by her shoulders, my grip tight, vice-like digging into her flesh, "Ah! Ow! Emil! You're hurting me!" She's finally awake, her face furrowed in confusion.

"Victoire! Get dressed, now!" My command is loud and deep. Her eyes widen and she begins to move from the bed, no questions asked. Fear sweeps her face when we hear car doors slamming shut, we both race to the closet. We had a plan in place, just for this instance. The night we talked about my father's letter I had thought about Victoire's suggestion that we leave, but I didn't want to run, I didn't want to allow Jäger or my father to scare us off. I wanted to stay where I knew I could protect Victoire, I needed to stay for my patients, but that didn't stop us from putting together a few things in case we had to flee. Victoire had packed a bag with warm clothes for both of us and placed out shoes that would help us through tough terrain. Thankfully, Victoire was a citizen of the world at one point and had hiking boots and a warm shearling coat. We begin to dress swiftly in the dark.

Bang! Bang! Bang!, the door.

We dress faster.

"Do you have the package," I ask her trying not to let my voice tremble." Victoire's breathing is erratic, holding back sobs as I hear her patting her coat with her hands, searching.

"Yes."

Bang! Bang! Bang!

"Hehh!," I hear her panic, I reach for her and kiss her lips like it is the last time. Then I pull back, digging my fingers into her padded shoulders.

"Listen to me, mon Ange. I love you with my whole heart…"

Bang! Bang! Bang!

"Make your way to the kitchen and stay there. Listen only for my voice. If I call you to come to me, come. If I yell for you to run, then my darling you must run…" I kiss her again, and again.

"No," she cries "no Emil, I must wait for you, I won't leave without you," her sobs break my heart. The knot in my throat tries to prevent me from protesting her demand to stay by my side, but I fight past it.

"NO!, you must go!"

Bang! Bang! Bang!

Jäger's voice calls up to me.

"von Koniiiig!"

We move. The vestibule guards us from being seen coming down the stairs, I push Victoire towards the corridor leading to the kitchen. Just as she makes her way inside, the front door bursts open. The door leading to the foyer, where I stand is also no match. In the blink of an eye, I am surrounded by five SS, Jäger and my father.

Victoire

I STAND by the kitchen door straining to hear what is happening. The buzzing in my ears from the blood pumping through my veins makes it difficult to understand the muffled sounds. I calm myself, I will need all my wits about me. I cannot afford to panic or make the wrong move. I slow my breath, close my eyes and listen to the voices.

"Hello, Emil." *Jäger…silence.*

"Stand back boy, I will deal with my son," *Herr von Konig, Emil's father,* "I find that this situation I have given you is not working to our benefit. I have reports that you have been cavorting with your maid. Is this true?" *more silence,* "Your job was simply to come here, practice medicine and maintain the honor of our family name, instead I hear otherwise. You no longer have a practice here in Paris, as of now, you are a battalion medical officer. We will make our way to Berlin, your post will be assigned to you from there."

"You would do this to your own son? Is there not a trace of love or care in your heart?" *...Emil*

There is an echoing snarl and footsteps are shuffling.

"The very fact that I have come for you, says that I love you! Do you know the charge for Rassenmischung!? Do you know the shame you have brought on this family!? The very fact that you breathe says that I care! I would not have our family embarrassed as your friend embarrassed his own!"

"How dare you!" *Emil shouting*, "You smug, self-righteous son of a bitch!" I hear a loud slap, then a few chuckles follow.

"Did I raise you to speak to me this way? I did not permit your mutter to give you life for you to dishonor this family!" *his father snarls loudly,* "What I did give you was an opportunity to be a man, honor me and the life I have allowed you to lead, instead you continue...instead you insist on disappointing me...and now here we are! Honestly, son, I could give a damn who you fuck, but when who you fuck begins to cost me my name and my business, it's time to draw the line."

"Search, the house!" Jäger's voice rings loud and clear. I back up from the door, waiting to hear Emil's command.

Emil

MY FATHER'S words do their job and hit me hard, so hard I almost don't register Jäger's command until one of the soldier's steps from his place towards the corridor.

"VICTOIRE! RUUUNN!" My hand goes to the throat of the soldier slamming him against the wall swiftly, blocking the pathway of the two advancing. I move my hand from around his neck and in the next split second, I grab his gun, already poised to shoot, and fire off two shots into the approaching men. *Three remaining and Jäger.* My father's eyes are wide as I wield the gun in his direction. As we stare each other down, I hear footsteps running toward the kitchen. They must have bypassed me and gone past the opposite side of the staircase, through the dining room which leads to the kitchen. I turn to run down the corridor. It's still dark, so I don't see the soldier that waits at the kitchen entrance. He hits me in the shoulder with his weapon, no doubt intending to strike me in the head. I grimace, but my mind overrides the pain. Bringing my gun across my body wildly, I pummel his face and neck, the bones crack in his nose. I strike forward to his chest with the sole of my boot. A sharp breath escapes him as he falls backward through the kitchen door. I stomp him quickly in the stomach, then bring the butt of my gun down on his forehead. I run to the back door. Jäger and the last two soldiers are at the edge of Victoire's garden plot, only meters from the woods.

"After her!!!!" Jäger screams, banshee-like into the early morning darkness. I can't see Victoire. My heart, already pounding out of my chest, doubles its work with panic. My eyes adjust, as I see one of the two remaining soldiers take off into the woods running at breakneck speed, with his MP34 swinging back and forth in his hands. I run up behind the soldier standing next to Jäger. Reaching out, I wrap his head in the triangle of my arm and pull around with all my strength, snapping his neck. *Jäger is next.* But, before I can lay my hands on him, I hear rapid shots fire in the woods, my eyes catch the faint light of tiny sparks. *No!* My heart rips in two.

"VICTOOIIIRREEE!" A heavy thud hits the back of my head. Darkness.

29

LITTLE RABBIT

In the woods
Behind a manor on the countryside
There is a light in the darkness

THE HOME OF HERR VON KONIG

Victoire

The very moment I hear Emil yell for me to run, my legs obey his command. I want to stay and fight, but I promised him that I would run. He made me promise not to wait, not to hesitate, only listen to the sound of his voice and do what he says. So, I do it. My hands push the back door wide open with a force so great the pressure cracks my wrists, then I sprint toward the woods.

We hadn't planned this far ahead, both of us subconsciously denying that anything would get this far. Yes, we had clothes ready, yes we had our little package ready, but that's all, that's as far as we'd gotten. No path, no *this is who you should run too*, nothing. As the days passed, and time grew further and further away from the day Emil received the letter from his father, we began to relax. Emil began to figure that his father's visit would be no more than a "hello, goodbye" and some light arguing in between. Instead, his father showed up unexpectedly at 5 o'clock in the morning with Jäger and several SS in tow.

I run.

My coat is heavy, and it's dark, too dark. My hands smack at tree limbs. My feet, boot laden, trip over tree roots and scattered mounds of snow, but I maintain my footing. Over my loud panting breaths, I hear Jäger shouting,

"After Herrrr!"

Like Lot's wife, I look back, a mistake I should not have repeated, instead of turning into a pillar of salt, I trip over a log and propel forward onto my stomach knocking the wind out of myself. I would have preferred the pillar of salt transformation. I roll around in pain, grabbing my waist, unable to breathe. I roll to my back, my eyes bulging, finally being forced to adjust to the light of the early morning moon. I hear the soldier's footsteps growing near, so I lay as still as I can hoping he won't see where I've landed.

A noise, no louder than the snap of a twig sounds off next to my ear, then a small object flies through the air. I hear the soldier's footsteps turn in the direction of the airborne article when it lands, he stops and shoots his gun rapidly.

"VIICTOOOOIRE!!"

I hear Emil scream for me in the distance. The pain in his voice sits like an anvil on my chest. I open my lips to yell for him, but just then a tiny little hand grabs my wrist. My open lips form an 'o', and without having to look, I know it is my

Little Rabbit. The smiling little boy that waits for me to enter the kitchen early mornings to sneak away loaves of warm bread and jam. I don't think, I just get up and run, letting his tiny cold hand lead me away to his home, deep in the woods.

30

BREAKING CAMP

Up a tall hill
On the edge of a camp
A little boy introduces his friend

A RESISTANCE CAMP DEEP IN THE WOODS

Victoire

The light is beginning to break. We must have been walking for an hour or more. *Is this how far my little one had to walk for a loaf of bread?* My heart sinks, and I begin to admonish myself for not giving him more, how could I have been so selfish? I slept warmly at night and had the comfort of eating any hot or cold meal I made for Emil while my Little Rabbit walked what might have been a kilometer or more to just eat a portion of what I feed Emil in a day. The tears well in my eyes, until his little face turns to me with a proud smile. Sunken, yet ruddy cheeks puff out like tiny red balloons. His brown eyes sparkle behind long wispy lashes and a giggle escapes him. The tears flow from me now not because of the guilt but because it is the first time in the year or so that we've been playing our little game that I've heard his voice. His laughter is sweet, a balm I didn't know I needed until this very moment, it shoots through my soul. I wiggle my wrist out of his grasp and replace it with my hand, his little palm only taking up half of my own. We walk this way up a giant hill. Once we reach the top, I look down and am amazed by what I see. It is a small village of tiny makeshift huts, small barely blazing fires, and people...so many people, milling around laughing, talking, bartering. I step forward and hear the clicking of several guns at my back. I freeze, then think of my Little Rabbit. I turn, pulling him behind me to protect him. He struggles a bit, but I do my best to keep him at my back.

"Lapin, attendez," [*Rabbit, wait*] I call to him as he breaks free and runs to break through the line of men holding up their guns, ready to shoot me. He pushes at one of the men who looks down irritated, but moves over making a hole for him. My Little Rabbit returns through the hole holding the hand of a man in grey clothes. My mind flashes back, *I'm under the cottage,* my eyes blink quickly to adjust, *the door is opening,* I shake my head to clear my mind, *the man in the woods says to get down,* then I realize he is the one who saved my life from the soldiers that day at my cottage. I rush to him, embracing him tightly. He does not return the embrace at first, though I know he remembers me by the way his eyes widened when he saw me, I don't feel his warmth until my Little Rabbit speaks.

"Papa, c'est la gentille dame, celle qui me donne du pain et des livres, et ces vilains légumes." [*Daddy, she's the nice lady, the one who gives me bread and books, and those ugly vegetables.*]

All the men laugh. His father wraps his hands around my arms and pushes me back to get a better look at me.

"Vraiment!?" [*Really!?*] he says with a smile.

"Elle est jolie n'est-ce pas, Je t'ai dit que j'avais une copine," [*She's pretty isn't she, I told you I had a girlfriend*] the men laugh at my Little Rabbit again, this time lowering their weapons.

"Yes, she is very pretty David, but don't tell your mother I said so," he wags his finger at the little boy. *David*. I whisper his name on my lips, never to forget it, and smile. His father continues his campaign, "You are too young for a girlfriend, besides I believe your friend Nina would be none too pleased to find your affections have been placed elsewhere, hmmm?" David's father gives him a mischievous grin. David kicks at a tiny lone mound of snow and looks up to me with a smile.

"You're very pretty, and I love your bread and jam...buuut Nina reads with me and she's teaching me how to add big numbers, sooo..." his beautiful little voice trails off as his grin grows wider. I bend down to him, eye to eye.

"I understand, David. Nina is a very lucky girl to have you as her friend. I hope one day to meet someone as brave, smart and handsome as you to bake bread for." David smiles, kisses me on the cheek then runs off down the hill to the camp. I turn back to his father whose face is now more serious after the departure of his son. He looks me over, head to toe.

"I do remember you. I've often wondered if you were alive. We had been staking out your cottage for days, making sure it was empty before we raided it, but the day we decided to move, is when we saw you and those Nazi bastards. You were lucky you fled from the house when you did. Elden snuck around front and smashed out their head-lights to give you time...whether you were there or not we would have opened fire. I'm sorry I couldn't stay to see if you were still under the cottage and alive, they had already killed two of our men, we couldn't risk more." He begins walking down the hill, I follow leaving the other men behind. They move back to what must have been their hidden posts. I follow in silence as he heads to a hut further to the back of the camp.

He opens the makeshift door, and as a gentleman he gestures for me to enter first. I walk in to see a small burning lamp, a few mismatched pots and pans, two short handmade stools and three blankets each lying on the floor. My heart wrenches.

"Please sit," he says. Just then, in rushes a beautiful woman, with wavy chestnut hair, pinned up in a bun. Her mouth is open, and her eyes shoot from me to the man in grey. She strides to me and without a word wraps her arms around me in a tight hug. I don't understand the hug, but it's warm and real so I take it and return it in kind.

"I am Lily, and this is my husband Ascher, we made a soup." I blink my eyes, not understanding what she means.

"I'm sorry?" I say shaking my head slowly. She laughs.

"The basket of vegetables that David brought home this summer, we made a soup and fed a few of our neighbors, and the bread and butter and jam, we take half and feed others or barter it," she kisses my hands and whispers a tear-filled, "Thank you."

"Why have you come?" Ascher asks unceremoniously with an edge in his voice.

"Ascher!" Lily scolds him. "Please, please sit." She moves me to one of the small wooden stools, and with that simple gesture I dissolve into sobs. From meeting my Little Rabbit, to the warmth of Lily's hand, to the makeshift home, the half of my heart I have left explodes, and I tell them everything that happened this morning. At the end of my story, Ascher is silent, rage in his eyes.

"How could you take up with a Nazi!" His words slap me in the face. This is not something I haven't beaten myself for time and again, but the moment I see Emil's face, the moment I smell his cologne or feel his touch, the thought floats away.

"I didn't plan it, he saved me. I was being rounded up. I had come home to Paris from the countryside to fetch my parents, but they were gone. I was running to try and make it to the Metro but just steps away I was stopped. They were stripping away my clothes in the street, pulling at my arms and hair like I was nothing, like I was an animal, then out of nowhere there he was–him and his friend Rolf. He took me to his home and claimed me as his maid." The tears return as I speak, my nose runs, and I wipe it on the sleeves of my coat. "He was a surgeon in the city, he never harmed a hair on my head, or anyone else, I promise." I clamp my hands together, pleading my case. "We planned to escape, but when his father showed up early this morning..." I double over weeping furiously, "He thinks I'm dead! Please, pleeeease, you must help me!"

"Ascher," Lily calls softly, "can you not help her?" Ascher furrows his brow.

"Help her? Help her save her Nazi lover!?" I shoot up from the stool and make my way to the door. "Where are you going," he shouts, rushing to the door before I can get there.

"I'm going to go save Emil!" Ascher laughs in my face.

"How!?...With what!?," he doesn't wait for my answer, though I have none, "Not only that, I won't let you compromise the location of this camp. These people are safe here. Who's to say that soldier my son saved you from in the woods, didn't follow you or isn't waiting for you to return to your home? How can I trust you won't tell them where you've been, who you've seen?" I begin to tremble with fear, not fear of bodily harm, but fear that I will never see Emil again, fear that Ascher won't let me leave this camp, much less go find my love. I try to push him aside to reach the door but he is heavy and built like a stone.

"Let me out," I scream and snarl, spit flying from my mouth, rabid. "Let me out," I scratch and hit at him, he grabs my arms shaking me. Suddenly, Lily pushes me aside and slaps Ascher across the face.

"Has it been that long Ascher!?" she screams, "Has it been that long, that you have forgotten how to treat a woman? Have you forgotten how to be human! Have you!?" I bury my face in her neck, giant sobs wrack my body. Her voice lowers as she strokes my hair, "Have you forgotten kindness and compassion Ascher?" She pulls my face back from her neck, her hands cradle my face and she looks me deep in my eyes as she speaks to him, "this woman has kept our little boy fed for a year, barely a day has gone by that there hasn't been something in his belly and a smile on his face. He and his friend Nina read to each other from the books she has gifted him. You have gone on missions that cost lives for causes less worthy. Not two weeks ago Simonne's son was shot dead over a mioir [*mirror*]...what was that worth? She asks you to save a life and you fight her!?"

"A Nazi!"

"A life!" Lily yells back, "Don't you see she is dying Ascher? Her heart is broken, obviously, this man has given her something more than just shelter. If not for him Ascher, for her...she sustained our little boy, at the very least you could sustain her."

Ascher looks at his beautiful wife, she has made her way to him, her hand on his cheek, her thumb caressing him, and he melts in her hand. With a giant sigh, he turns to me.

"We tell no one who we are going on this mission for," I nod my head rapidly, clasping my hands together thanking him and Lily profusely, "Tell me where they are taking him."

I wrack my brain going back over the bellows and yelling from Emil's father, but I can't remember, *I must,* I dig deeper, slowing my mind, even using the alphabet to help jog my memory. Sounds, colors, movements flash before me, *it's there - it's there; try harder.* The door bursts open and in runs little David with a toy in his hand. He giggles and runs into my knees, placing his little hands on my thighs.

"Ow," I whisper, I look down and see David pressing a worn, paint chipped tiny toy train into my flesh, my mind snaps, "they are taking him to Berlin and demoting him to a battalion doctor!" I jump from my stool, my heart racing ready to go.

Ascher places his hand on my shoulder and lowers me back down gently grinning widely, "there are only two trains still running from Paris to Germany, the one in the morning is for the Führer himself, the second one at night is for the mice, that is where your Emil will be. We wait here until nightfall. God may be on your side after all madame."

31

MISSION

On the Parisian countryside
On a very cold wrought iron bench
A broken hearted lover awaits his fate

A RURAL TRAIN STATION

Emil

The cold seeps into my bones, and my body aches. My head pounds mercilessly. The butting of the gun against the back of my head knocked me out cold. I don't know who did it, Jäger or my Father. In all honesty, I'd rather not know. One I would kill, the other I'm not sure, but it'd be a bad situation on both accounts. I pull myself together, I'm about to think of Victoire again, and I can't...I just can't, each time I do, all I see are the gunshots. I can't decide whether she made it or if she didn't. Did I give her enough time to run? Should I have told her to run as soon as they banged on the door? She's gone and my mind, my heart can't fathom the loss. The last time I thought of her, not minutes ago, I passed out— my brain's way of blocking the pain. I can't afford to do it again. I fight the tears pushing at my eyes incessantly. God! Why didn't I tell her to run sooner? Why didn't I make her go! I can't fight it, the tears come and I grit my teeth against the sting, against the pain in the back of my head, against my body's coping mechanism to pass out again. I feel heat at my side.

Jäger sits next to me grinning. My arms are cuffed behind my back. *Smart*, I can't reach out and strangle him like I want to.

"Your little black whore is dead," he grins, crossing his legs. He removes a glove and places his hand in his pocket pulling out a silver case. After a few moments, the scent of German tobacco enters my nostrils, a smell that used to be sweet, but now turns my stomach. "She's alone in the woods...her body is cold now. Her legs are spread wide for any animal to take her," he chuckles when I try to free my hands from the cuffs to kill him. "Now-- now calm down. I'm sure many of the animals will pass her over until morning, she's too dark for them to see right now anyway. Though I would have liked to have tried my hand at her before they did, you ruined my chance, so I'll just have to go out and find a random stag and ask him how she was," he laughs again, "Then I'll shoot him, cut off his head and place him on my wall...a double trophy, ja!"

"Fuck you, Jäger. You wanted her the moment you saw her on the street, that's what all this is about. The desires of your tiny, useless dick," it's my turn to chuckle, but when I do I feel the sting of his leather glove swat across my face, I chuckle harder. Jäger rears back his fist,

"Jäger!" My father's voice carries on the gentle breeze I feel pushing forward through the trees from the approaching train, still more than a kilometer out yet. Jäger drops his fist. He stands to leave, but thinks, turning back to me and bending low.

"One day soon we'll meet again you gilded, arrogant, fuck. On that day your money, your Vati's connections, your prestige as a surgeon won't help you. It's only too sad your luscious Victoire won't be there as a spoil for the victor."

I keep my face forward, gnashing my teeth, "I'll be waiting." The breeze increases, freezing the moisture on my cheek. My father begins to saunter over, but his head turns when a series of whistles begin to float through the air. They stop and he looks around. I furrow my brows, not sure what to think of what I've heard. He continues to walk toward me. The whistles grow closer and are now followed by high trills that seem to leap from one end of the track to the other.

I see the smoke from the train approaching, then I see two guards at the far end of the track fall over, hitting the ground, their helmets making distant clanging noises. I sit up and squint my eyes to see more clearly. I turn to the other side of the track, straining my neck to see around my father, and view another set of guards lying prostrate on the ground. Light from the train comes into view as it rounds the corner. I turn straight ahead and see ten men with guns running in my direction, *Resistance.* A multi-voiced, loud roaring yell comes from the direction of the men. I smile to myself, *if this is how I die, then sobeit,* gunshots ring out, as soldier after unsuspecting soldier is hit. There aren't many here tonight, so the Resistance has a field day of it. My father picks up a gun from a fallen guard, wields it in the air and is shot straight through the chest. My heart lurches for a moment, then the moment passes as quickly as it came. I wish I felt more, but I don't. I remain seated awaiting my turn to die, to be with Victoire, but a large rough set of hands grabs at my shoulders, shaking my eyes open.

"Are you Emil!" My eyes widen and shoot back and forth at the faces in front of me, I don't know what to say, he shakes me hard and asks again "ARE. YOU. EMIL!?"

"Yes!" The man beckons for one of his comrades to come over, he whispers in his ear and the man takes off a few steps away, then returns with a set of keys. While he is reaching behind me to try and unlock my wrists, the man who asked my name yells at me over the commotion.

"You come with me! Ask no questions! Do not speak! We have no time to waste!" The train whistles as it descends upon us. Jäger runs out of the depot just as we jump onto the train tracks. My hands break free as I roll. When I stand to run I see Jäger aiming his pistol at me, I brace myself just as the train roars between us, the force pushes me backward into the arms of the man with the rough hands. "We must go, NOW! MOVE!"

I do as he says, asking no questions, not speaking a word and moving as fast as I can. We run like a herd of deer deep into the woods, deep into the night.

Victoire

I WAIT in the clearing with three of Ascher's men. My nerves are bad, thinking of everything that could go wrong, wondering how long it has been since Ascher and his men left, wanting each and every one of them to come back safely — wanting Emil to be with them. Nervous, I wring my hands, then check my pocket for the package making sure it's there and tucked tight. Minutes later I check again. I'm going crazy.

"It's been too long, it's been too long," I cry to one of the men. He puts his hand on my shoulder and without a word, simply shakes his head back and forth, then he points straight ahead. In the moonlight I see the rustling of brush, then the tops of heads, then faces...then the loveliest face of all, Emil. I see him, he sees me and we run at breakneck speed until we collide.

Emil let's out a deep, moaning sob into the crook of my neck. I am strong for him as he is a boy again in this moment, lamenting a heartache, crying out for his mother to come save him in the night. I hold him tight, giving him gentle shuush's in his ear, stroking his corn silk hair, a baby in the body of a man.

"Victoire--- Victoire" is all he can say, and it is enough.

"Shhh, Autrichien, sshhhh, I am here." He pulls back from me, running his hands over my face, cradling it, then running his hands over me again, "I am here Emil, it is not a dream." We kiss passionately, tasting each other's tongues like it is the first time, sweet and briny. He breaks the kiss leaning his forehead down on mine.

"I thought you were dead. They told me you were dead. I am a shell without you, Victoire." We are about to kiss again when Ascher interrupts us. He is followed by a man who is breathing heavily.

"You must go, now! Moise has just seen a troop heading this way about a kilometer out. You must listen carefully. There is a man with a plane, it is small but may fit you both. He keeps it hidden in a barn but for the right price, he can fly you anywhere you want to go." Emil and I look at each other and nod. Emil the man is back now, the little boy has gone within.

"In which direction do we go?"

"I will send Moise with you to guide you. I sent word ahead this afternoon, he will be expecting you." Emil reaches out his hand to Ascher, and for a moment Ascher only stares at it, but then he accepts it giving Emil a firm head nod. I move from Emil's side and hug Ascher with all my might.

"Thank you, Ascher, and please give all my love to Lily and my Little Rabbit, David." Ascher nods, we begin to follow Moise, when Emil turns back.

"I can never repay you this debt. Until the day I can, here is the key to the car; it's yours. Use it for whatever you need, parts, shelter anything, the cottage and the house, please use them, the pantries are both stocked, warm clothes and blankets, liquor and wood for days." Ascher takes the key and smiles.

"My men are already there," he chuckles out. Emil smiles slapping Ascher on the shoulder. He takes my hand, and we follow Moise into the night.

3 2

FLIGHT

On the Run
Jäger on one side
A plane on the other

A BARN ON THE PARISIAN COUNTRYSIDE

Emil

Moise left us to try and hold off the smaller band of soldiers that had broken away from the larger troop and flanked us. As gunfire sounds off in the distance, Victoire and I bang desperately on the barn door where we were told the man with the plane would be waiting. He rolls the door back and there in front of us is salvation, a four-seat single engine plane. He looks at us both, scowling and shaking his hand 'no'.

"I expected you hours ago, and now you bring trouble to my door, no. Go away, now!" He tries to close the barn door, but I use all my strength to hold it open.

"Please, please," I call to him, *I cannot fail Victoire again.* "Please just take her, it's not her fault, it was me, I made us late, please!" I grab Victoire around the waist, hoisting her over my shoulder then force myself past the man who is visibly shaken by my height and determination.

Victoire screams hitting my back with her fists, kicking violently.

"No! No! I will not go without you, NO!!!" The man follows behind. More shots ring out.

"It's not about the amount of people, it's the trouble you have brought me. I do this and I can never return, do you hear me?"

Something in me compels me to ask, "Do you have a family? A lover?" The man's mouth sits agape, he cannot answer, because the answer is 'no'. "Please." I look him in the eye, willing him to say 'yes'. He looks around his barn longingly, already making his decision.

"I need my pay upfront." I set Victoire on her feet, the gunshots quiet, but now we can hear the whirring of engines.

I nod to Victoire, "The package, mon Ange, quickly." She pulls out the white handkerchief, with trembling fingers, she kneels to the floor trying her best to open it as the engines grow closer, I run to the barn door and see headlights. "Do you have a gun?" The man nods his head over to the wall where a rifle sits on a rack. I check the chamber and make sure it's loaded. "Victoire, dépêchez-vous!" [*Victoire, hurry!*]

Victoire opens the package finally dumping out every-thing, our passports, money- over 100 francs, a picture of Rolf in case Victoire made her way back to Marrakech, two cyanide tablets and Rolf's signet ring...everything we owned in the world. The man swoops down on the francs, and the signet ring, bringing it to his teeth and biting it to confirm the matter as pure gold. The lights grow brighter as I wait at the barn door.

"We need to push the plane out, I'll need your help!" I run to the plane, passing Victoire who is putting Rolf's picture, the passports and tablets back into the breast pocket of her coat. She runs to my side and helps to push. *My woman.*

The plane is out of the barn and on the wet snowy ground. I make sure Victoire is in the plane and seated before I run back for the gun I dropped at the door. I hear the propeller engine roar to life as the headlights of one vehicle bare down on the plane, *Jäger*. Two other utility vehicles trail far behind at the clearing of the tree line.

Jäger appears, jutting up and balancing his body precariously through the top of the roof,

"HAAAAALT!"

Victoire

FROM THE WINDOW of the plane, I see Jäger and Emil aim at each other…

33

BYE-BYE FOR NOW

On a Settee
Late in the afternoon
A mother and daughter await their tea

CALIFORNIA | 1980

Lily

My mother's words trail off until she is silent. I watch her as she stares longingly through the window again. I wonder if she is watching her life-like pictures in a movie through the panes of glass.

"Maman?" I call to her quietly as I place my hand on hers, a hand that through the years has remained so soft and warm, a glowing shade of fresh pecans only showing signs of age by the now prominent veins that pump her brave blood, "Maman, are you okay", she turns her brown almond-shaped eyes to me and smiles.

"Oui Chérie, Je vais bien," [*Yes Dear, I'm fine*] she covers my hand with both of hers "the story is finished," I smile at her and furrow my brow in disbelief.

"Are you sure?" I prod a little bit more and giggle as she nods slowly with a shy smile.

"Bien sûr, you know the rest." Just as she assures me, there is a low knock at the door. When it opens the smell of tea and honey cake fill my nostrils with delight. And in walks the most handsome man, my father. Tall and grey with eyes blue like the ocean, and a smile that has always brightened every dark moment in my life.

"I am sorry mon Ange. Forgive me, I am late with your tea. Your son Rolf chats incessantly on the phone." He lifts the tray and places it on the small serving table beside us. As usual, when he enters the room my father does not address me first. He always seeks Maman, giving her a gentle kiss on the temple, then whispering something in her ear to make her blush and smile. This is the way it's been my whole life. I've never asked Maman what it is that Vati whispers to her. I've just always known that I wanted that same type of love for myself when I grew up, which I found my third year in college. My husband is tall, beautiful with the most gorgeous dark chocolate skin and wavy hair, such a visual contrast to my father, but he looks at me and whispers to me like Vati does with Maman and that's all I ever wanted.

My father turns to me with a wide smile and a sparkle of mischief in his eye "Ah! Well hello, mein Klößchen!" [*my Dumpling!*] He always pretends that he's just noticing me or my siblings are in the room after whispering to my mother. When we were little it drove us crazy with giggles. He would walk around the room turning over chairs and lifting pillows calling our names, pretending he couldn't see us. Then he would look down and magically three little people would appear before his eyes. I remember thinking just in that moment, for the briefest of seconds, my father was over-whelmed with joy, there was often a fleeting glisten in his eyes that went away as instantly as it came; he never missed a beat, swooping down from his tall, muscled crane-like frame and scooping us into his arms. He'd shower us with hugs and kisses, wildly speaking to us in a rapid succession of German, English and French! My mother would yell to him "Autrichien, une langue à la fois." [*Austrian, one language at a time.*] He would ignore her and then whisper to us, continuing in all three languages--saying funny evil things, like "Mean Maman, we don't like her" or "Mommy wants you *aaaalll* to be dunderheads so you can stay home with her forever tugging at her skirts and eating up all her wonderful honey cakes, but I will not allow it. You must learn and be smart because I want her honey cakes all to myself!" And with a giant roar, there would be tickles and bites and giggles as he chased us through the house. There was rarely ever an unhappy moment in our home; it was like sadness just ceased to exist--they simply refused it, save only for a small period of time when I was very young.

I was four and my older brother Rolf was six, Ascher had not yet been born. I remember one day Vati was home with us, hugging and kissing us telling Rolf to watch over me and Maman because he was now the man of our home. The next morning, he was gone. I didn't see my father again until my sixth birthday. The days, weeks and months in between I asked Maman many times for my Vati. Her reply would come with a sullen stare off into a room behind us and she would begin to cry. Maman would tell me that my Vati was away being very brave for me and Rolf and one day I would under-stand, and that Vati loved us all so very much.

I stopped asking Maman because it hurt her so much, but finally, one day Vati just returned. He had the same smile and those deliciously evil jokes about Maman's honey cakes. Everything was put right again. Yes, he was a little thinner and there would be times when he would just sit silently with a saddened look in his ocean blue eyes, but those times were few and far between. Maman made sure his weight returned, then Ascher came along quickly after. It wouldn't be until my teens that I learned what had happened during those two years. Where Vati had gone and why. I choose not to think of his imprisonment, it hurts too much. And I would be remiss to say that I wasn't embarrassed and horrified back then, knowing that my Vati had not only turned himself over and gone to prison but that his incarceration was due to his participation in one of the most awful times in history. But, with age comes wisdom and with wisdom, forgiveness. I love my Vati.

"Komm und umarme mein Klößchen!" [*Come and hug me my Dumpling!*] I wobble myself up off of the small settee rubbing my eight month belly, feeling ready to pop. My father gives me a great bear hug as he kisses my temple.

"Careful mon Amour, she is with child," my mother admonishes.

"Yes, yes Leibchen, I have noticed. " He doesn't loosen his grip, and I don't want him to. "I hug her tight so the baby can feel love from his Gróßvater, ja!?" [*Grandfather, yes!?*]

"Yes, Vati," I answer with a giggle. He moves from his hug and dances me slowly in a half circle, then takes my hands and helps lower me back down gently to a sweet little armchair across from the settee. *Smooth Vati*. Now that he is here, his place is seated next to Maman...as always. I shake my head and smile.

"Und how is your husband treating you?"

I roll my eyes at his question.

"Vati, you just saw him last week, you know he treats me very well." My father smiles proudly.

"Yes, Klößchen, but a Father must always hear it from the mouth of his daughter, and see it in her eyes...und you are happy, I see it." I roll my eyes again smiling and looking down at my very pregnant belly, and I give it a few more rubs as I answer.

"Yes, Vati and Maman, I am very happy."

"Bon Chérie." My mother smiles at me, and absentmind-edly caresses my father's cheek.

"Oui! Wonderful, das ist schön!" he exclaims, looking at my mother out of the corner of his eye with a glint of mischief. He flinches with a giggle as he sees her hand moving to push him.

"One language at a time," she says playfully, giving him a gentle love tap on the shoulder, he catches her hand and brings it to his lips kissing it tenderly multiple times. They stare at each other for a moment, and in that moment, I can see them...young and in love, a fire between them that no one could quell. My mother reaches up her other hand to caress his face, and my father closes his eyes as if absorbing the feeling of her fingers against his skin. My eyes shoot back and forth between the two of them.

"Hggh-hghm, I clear my throat, and as if they were waking abruptly from a sweet dream they grin and look at me with impish smiles. "Well, I see it's time for me to go." They both feign protests for me to stay, but I'm not stupid, they've been this way for all my 29 years. I've known the signs since I was five. Nothing was ever lost on me, the middle child, their all-seeing little girl. I pick up my purse and smile while shaking my head at their continued faux battle for me to stay.

"Alright, alright Klößchen," my father says with a triumphant smile, "have Lisette give you some honey cake to take to your husband, ja...but before you go, have you two thought about any names yet?"

My heart leaps and I kick myself for forgetting to tell them, I've been so wrapped up in the story.

"We've decided on 'David', it's Hebrew meaning 'Beloved'." They look at me with such intense love. Their grandchild carrying a name that speaks so loudly of their love story. My husband and I had no idea when we'd chosen it--I can't wait to tell him when I get home. My father's eyes begin to water, and his tears trickle sweetly down his reddened cheeks.

"Oh, Vati, noo, no...please don't cry." I waddle to him and press his head tenderly against my protruding belly. He leans in and nuzzles me wiping away his tears, then places his large warm hand over his grandchild and whispers to him,

"I will see you soon, meine Klößchen."

THE END

THANK YOU

Thank you so much for reading my debut novel
Love and War.
Come and be a part of the Shirrá Lynn Romance family!
Follow me on Facebook, and Instagram, then visit my
website to sign-up for exclusive news and updates!
Oh! Don't forget to head over to my Spotify to listen to my
playlist that helped inspire the love story between Emil and
Victoire!

ABOUT THE AUTHOR

Shirrá Lynn is a native of Washington, DC. A writer of Inter-racial Romance, she is also a hobbyist poet and floral designer. When she isn't writing or snipping roses, she loves spending time with her family, especially her nieces and nephew. In college, during a critique session in a creative writing class, her professor described her writing style as 'too colloquial'. Shirrá took this appraisal and used it as a catalyst to produce stories that are engaging, real and speak to the heart.

'Love and War' is her debut romance novel.